TERMINAL

ALSO BY MARSHALL KARP

THE LOMAX AND BIGGS MYSTERIES

Cut, Paste, Kill

Flipping Out

Bloodthirsty

The Rabbit Factory

COAUTHORED WITH JAMES PATTERSON

NYPD Red 4

NYPD Red 3

NYPD Red 2

NYPD Red

Kill Me If You Can

For details and sample chapters please visit www.karpkills.com

TERMINAL

A Lomax and Biggs Mystery

Marshall Karp

ISBN-10: 1523821000
ISBN-13: 978-1523821006

Jacket design by Dennis Woloch
Book design by Kathleen Otis
Author photo by Fran Gormley

For information email contact@karpkills.com

AN OVERLY LONG, POSSIBLY OVERWRITTEN DEDICATION

***This book is dedicated** with love and gratitude to every Lomax and Biggs fan on the planet. You may be a few thousand whackos short of a cult following, but you are annoyingly, wonderfully, and magically persistent.*

After Cut, Paste, Kill was published in 2010, you waited for Lomax and Biggs 5. But the publishing business is a not-too-subtle balance of art and commerce, and commerce almost always kicks art's ass.

So like Willie Sutton, my career told me to go where the money was. I co-authored five best sellers with James Patterson, and while most of you understood, you still wanted me to find time for Lomax and Biggs. And you were not shy in your communication. On Facebook, on Twitter, on Goodreads, and of course, email. Lots and lots of email. Sometimes you were gentle. Please, Marshall... But other times you were just a bunch of book junkies jonesing for your next Lomax and Biggs fix.

I knew it would take years, but I couldn't say no. And when I finally started writing this book, I realized I missed Mike Lomax, Terry Biggs, Big Jim, Diana, Muller, and Kilcullen as much as you did. I also wanted to develop the newest character, Sophie Tan, the seven-year-old who was left in Mike and Diana's care at the end of Cut, Paste, Kill. In Terminal, Sophie comes into her own—a wise-beyond-her-years force to be reckoned with. I must admit, I've fallen in love with this kid, and hope you will too.

Terminal has been a labor of love, and when the time came to think of a dedication, I didn't have to think twice. I couldn't name names. The list would go on for pages. And I knew I wouldn't be able to live with myself if I left one out.

But you know who you are. More important, I know who you are.

Thank you.

PROLOGUE

AMATEUR HOUR

ONE

THE PRIUS IDLED in total silence. The hybrid was so damn quiet that even when it was barreling down the road a pedestrian could barely hear it coming.

Which, of course, was part of the plan.

Bruce Bower angled the driver's seat so he could lean back and look through the moon roof. Not much moon to be looked at—just a sliver of white that did little to light the quiet suburban LA street. That too was part of the plan.

He stared heavenward and thought about his life—the fifty-one years that had gone by and the four to six weeks Dr. Spang said he had left. He smiled.

"What's so funny?" Claire asked.

He adjusted the seat so he could see her face in the faint glow that came through the windshield. Thirty-one years since he fell in love with her, and she was still beautiful, still sexy, still everything he ever desired.

"I was just thinking how I spent my entire career dispensing brilliant tax advice," Bruce said, "and now your entire financial future rests on where some dog decides to take a crap."

"Dogs are creatures of habit," Claire said. "Last night was a fluke. Tonight he'll get it right."

It all hinged on a five-year-old yellow Lab named Maverick.

Bruce and Claire had done three test runs. Every night

between ten and eleven, Wade Yancy would open the front door of his house at 476 Comstock Avenue, and Maverick would come bounding out, a flashing blue LED safety light hooked to his collar.

Three out of three times the dog headed for the opposite side of the street, stopped at the bend in the road, and did his business directly in front of somebody else's four-million-dollar home.

Yancy would follow with a glass of wine in one hand and a pooper-scooper bag in the other. He'd crouch down to pick up the shit, because that's the kind of thoughtful neighbor Wade Yancy was. But half-drunk and with his back to the oncoming traffic, he was an accident waiting to happen.

All Bruce had to do was put the car in gear, come around the blind turn doing forty, and the deadly silent Prius would do the rest.

Last night was supposed to be the night, but the dog never crossed the street. Maverick had opted to take a quick piss up against a tree on Yancy's property and went back into the house for the night.

That might be the kind of setback a professional killer could deal with, but not Claire. As soon as Yancy closed his front door, she started to cry. Bruce did his best to comfort her, but in the end, he cried along with her.

They went home, drank wine, made love, and did the only thing they could do. They pushed the murder off another day. Again, not much of a setback for a professional, but Bruce didn't have that many days left.

It was now twenty-four hours and fifteen minutes since the aborted attempt, and Bruce reached for the pack of Luckies sitting on the dashboard.

"Do you think that's such a good idea?" Claire said.

"I thought it was," he said, picking up the cigarettes, "but judging by the verbal topspin you put on the words *good* and *idea*, you think it's anything but."

"Very perceptive. I've got Nicorette gum in my purse. You want some?"

"Nicorette is for people who are trying to quit smoking. I'll quit for good soon enough. Until then, I have Dr. Spang's blessings to smoke like a Chevy Vega. I am no longer a gum chewer, Claire. I'm a Stage IV smoker."

"You're also a Stage IV asshole," Claire said. "Do you really think I'm trying to stop you from smoking? I'm only afraid that if you light up, somebody could see us sitting here."

"Oh," he said, putting the cigarettes back on the dash.

She reached into her purse and pulled out a square of Nicorette. "Chew this. You can smoke all you want when the cops get here."

"This reminds me of our third date," he said, chomping down on the mint-flavored wad of nicotine-infused rubber and resting a hand on her thigh.

She covered his hand with hers and kissed his cheek. "Don't get too horny, lover boy, because there are things I could do in the front seat of a car when I was twenty that I can't do now."

"I'm not talking about the sex," he said. "Third date was the first time you started bossing the shit out of me, and you haven't stopped since."

"Have I told you lately that you're an asshole?" she said, punching him gently on the shoulder.

"Stage IV," he said. He was about to return the kiss when she sat up straight.

"The door's opening," she said.

They watched as the flashing blue light loped across the street and headed for the curve in the road.

"Good doggie," Bruce said.

The light stopped moving, and the dog circled, looking for the perfect piece of Holmby Hills real estate to leave his mark.

"Poop is now in progress," Claire said in a mock robotic voice.

Bruce had one hand on the steering wheel, the other on the

gearshift. "Get your cell phone ready," he said.

Claire removed the phone from her purse, never taking her eyes off the flashing blue light that was the only insurance policy her dying husband had.

The dog finished and scampered off to piss in the bushes, leaving the pile of shit for his multimillionaire owner to deal with.

"Mr. Yancy has had a few," Claire said.

"More than a few," Bruce said as he watched his prey stumble off the curb and weave his way across the street.

As soon as Yancy squatted down, Bruce put the car in gear and hit the gas.

"Be careful you don't hit the dog," Claire warned.

"The dog doesn't deserve to die," Bruce said as the Prius accelerated from zero to forty in 5.3 seconds. "Yancy does."

They had done their research. Thirty was the speed limit on Comstock, but a pedestrian who might survive being hit at thirty would be roadkill at forty.

The headlights were out, but Bruce had no trouble honing in on the two-hundred-fifty-pound target. And then, as if God had decided that Claire and Bruce Bower had waited for closure long enough, Yancy stood up, and the front bumper of the Prius struck him at knee level, pummeling bones, blood vessels, and tissue.

As soon as he heard the thud, Bruce hit the brakes, but the laws of kinetic energy were still in control. The forward motion continued, and the hood of the car connected with Yancy's pelvis, and his body went airborne, landing on a lawn sixty feet away.

Bruce turned on the headlights before the Prius even came to a stop.

"Oh my God," he screamed. "Claire, I hit somebody, I hit somebody."

They had decided that scripting a story wasn't enough. Acting it out and living it in real time would make the lies much more believable.

Claire immediately went into character and dialed 911.

Bruce sat behind the wheel, dazed, numb. "I never saw him," he said. "He came out of nowhere."

"See if he's okay," Claire yelled. She turned to her phone. "My name is Claire Bower. We just hit someone with our car. I don't know—just a minute. Bruce, where the hell are we?"

"Comstock Avenue," he yelled. "Somewhere between Beverly Glen and Sunset, but closer to Beverly Glen. It wasn't my fault. He came out of nowhere."

Bruce threw the car door open and ran toward the body yelling, "I'm sorry. I'm sorry. I never saw you." He was immersed in the part now, and by the time the paramedics arrived, he was confident that his blood pressure would be through the roof.

The dog was on all fours, whimpering, nuzzling Yancy's face, trying to get a response.

Bruce knelt down in the grass next to the body. "I'm sorry," he said, first to the broken, bloodied man on the ground, and then again to the dog.

"The police will be here in three minutes," Claire yelled, getting out of the car and walking toward him. "Is he okay? Please tell me he's okay."

"I don't know," Bruce yelled back. "Hold on." He pulled his cell phone from his pocket and turned on the flashlight. Yancy's eyes were glazed over, locked in the thousand-yard stare.

Bruce made the official pronouncement. "He's dead."

"Are you sure?" Claire said, real tears streaming down her cheeks. "Maybe he's still breathing."

She dropped to her knees and pressed an ear to the dead man's chest.

A wet, gurgling moan erupted from Yancy's throat. Claire bolted backwards and screamed.

Yancy struggled to speak. "Call...nine...one...one," he implored.

She didn't have to. She could already hear the sirens in the distance.

TWO

"I CAN PRACTICALLY hear the wheels turning inside that head of yours," Claire said. "What are you thinking about?"

"I was just doing the math," Bruce said.

They were sitting on the back step of LAFD Rescue Ambulance 71. The paramedics had taken their vitals, determined they were well enough to be detained at the scene, and had run down the road to join the cops and firefighters congregating around Wade Yancy.

Despite the fact that no one could possibly hear her, Claire whispered. "The math? Honey, there's fifty thousand in the bank in the Caymans, and by this time tomorrow, there'll be another four fifty. Even I can figure that out."

"Not that math," Bruce said. "I'm trying to calculate what it's costing the city of Los Angeles to respond to the accident. LAPD sent four patrol units and a T car; LAFD has two engines, an ALS and a BLS rescue ambulance; there's a team from SID taking pictures, the ME just arrived, plus the DOT has a crew detouring traffic at both ends of Comstock Avenue—all for one simple Vehicle versus Ped."

"For God's sake, Bruce," she said in a harsh whisper. "Lose the cop lingo, or somebody will hear you and figure out that you researched every inch of this investigation a week before the accident happened."

He shook his head. "This is why I love you. I was sitting here quietly, but you had to know what I was thinking. I tell you, and I get yelled at."

"I just don't want you to screw it up."

"I haven't screwed anything up yet—probably because I did all that research. And just a reminder—you're the one crashing the party here. You're not supposed to even know what I'm doing, much less be a part of it. It's totally against their rules."

"*Their* rules? What about Thou Shalt Not Kill? They have no problem if you break that rule. What are they going to do if they find out I was with you—ask me for their money back?"

Bruce shrugged. "I don't know what they'll do, but whatever it is, that'll be the new guy's problem."

"What new guy?"

"You're young, you're beautiful, you'll have a nice little nest egg—trust me, there's going to be a new guy."

"I don't think so, Bruce. Thirty-one years of living on the edge with a wild and crazy high-flying accountant is all the excitement I can handle in one lifetime."

He laughed. "Oh yeah—that's me—the Evel Knievel of CPAs."

"That cop is coming back," Claire said. "Try to act like you're in shock."

"I am in shock," Bruce said. "I can't believe I earned a half-million dollars for a couple of hours work."

Officer Matt McCormick had stepped out of the circle surrounding Wade Yancy and was walking up the road to the ambulance.

"How are you folks holding up?" he said gently. He was only three years on the job, but he had a natural gift for bringing calm to the chaos of a sudden and violent traffic accident.

Claire smiled. "Thank you, Officer McCormick. We're doing better."

"Mr. Bower," McCormick said, "the paramedic told me your

BP was high, but that's normal in situations like this. I'd like you to take me through the accident, but if you don't feel well, the ambulance can take you to UCLA Med."

"I'm okay for now," Bruce said. "But EMS has been here awhile, and he's still lying there, so I guess he's..."

"Yes sir, I'm sorry to tell you that the victim has expired. If it's any consolation, the coroner is pretty sure he never suffered. He died on impact."

"On impact," Bruce repeated. "I guess that's some kind of a blessing."

"Does he have a family?" Claire asked.

"A wife and two teenage daughters."

"I heard screaming," Claire said.

"That was one of the girls. She's in shock. They took her back to the house. One of the paramedics is with her now." He took out a pad. "Mr. Bower, why don't you tell me what happened."

"We were home and decided to drive out to Century City for some ice cream," Bruce said. "We always cut across Comstock from Sunset to Beverly Glen—it's faster. So I know the road. I wasn't speeding. And I didn't have anything to drink. You can test me."

"That's okay, sir," McCormick said. "I can tell."

"We're driving on Comstock, and out of the corner of my eye I see this flashing blue light on the other side of the street. Even so, I didn't look away. Then all of a sudden this man just stands up—he's right in front of the car, but his back is to me. I never saw him. He never saw me."

"He probably never heard you either," McCormick said. "The NHTSA is trying to get laws passed to make these hybrids noisier, but it's too late for Mr. Yancy."

"Is that his name?" Claire asked.

"Yes ma'am. Wade Yancy, forty-seven years old," McCormick said. "Finish your story, Mr. Bower. You say he just stood up in front of you?"

"I don't understand," Bruce said. "Where did he come from?"

"The way we pieced it together, it looks like he was squatting on the roadway picking up after his dog and stood up just as you came around the curve. There was an empty wineglass on the shoulder at the point of impact. He must have set it down when he was cleaning up after the dog. I have no doubt that the tox report will show he was drinking."

Bruce shook his head. "What happens next?" he asked.

"I'll write up a report stating that the primary collision factor was the pedestrian, probably impaired, in the roadway, and if it hadn't been for him, there would not have been a collision. A traffic detective will be out here shortly, and if he signs off on it, which I'm confident he will, you're free to go. Your car is damaged, but one of the uniforms checked it out. It'll get you home. Are you okay to drive?"

"I'm fine," Bruce said.

"He's fine," Claire said. "But I'm driving."

"Good call, Mrs. Bower," McCormick said, giving her a big smile. "Anything else I can do for you while we're waiting for the detective?"

"Just one question," she said. "How do you do it?"

"Do what, ma'am?"

"You must see tragedies like this every day. How do you manage to stay so positive, so upbeat?"

"I don't have a choice. When I get to a scene, people are hurting—physically, emotionally, psychologically. I'm not there to add more pain to the mix. My job is to sort things out and bring comfort wherever I can."

"Well, you have. I only hope you don't go home after work and cry yourself to sleep."

"Don't worry about that, Mrs. Bower. The one thing you learn on this job is to enjoy life as much you can, because you never know what's going to sneak up on you and pull the plug on the whole deal."

His cell phone rang. He checked the caller ID and smiled. "Speaking of fun, it's my fiancé. Excuse me."

"The kid's right," Bruce said as soon as the cop was out of earshot. "You never know what's going to sneak up on you and pull the plug on the whole deal." He paused and smiled. "Like a Stage IV asshole in a Prius."

PART ONE

DIAGNOSIS

CHAPTER 1

I DID A quick head count as soon as I walked into the waiting room. Eight people waiting for the doctor. I walked to the receptionist's desk and printed my name on the sign-in sheet. There were spaces for *Time of Appointment* and *Time of Arrival*. I left them blank.

The glass window slid open, and Nadine smiled up at me. She had blue eyes, silver hair, and a deep whiskey-coated voice. No matter how sick you were when you walked into Dr. Heller's office, Nadine immediately made you feel better.

"Hello, handsome," she said. "And how are you today?"

"Fashionably late."

She looked at her watch. "Honey, an hour and twenty minutes ain't fashionable—even in LA."

"I was stuck at a crime scene. I called and left a message with somebody—I didn't catch her name."

"I know. Somebody, whose name is Helen, told me you were out fighting crime, and you'd get here when you got here." She leaned close to the window and whispered. "I think you just didn't want to come back here for that prostate exam."

"Doug gave me a complete physical last week. Head to toe."

"Minus one part," she said, wiggling a finger in the air.

"Not my fault. He stepped out of the office, I got a call from my lieutenant, and I had to race back to the station. I'm sorry

I couldn't stick around for Doug to come back, grease up, and work me like a sock puppet."

She let loose with a lung-butter laugh that sounded like the Roto-Rooter man was unclogging her pipes. People in the waiting room looked up, half smiles on their faces, hoping to be let in on the fun.

"Nadine, serious question," I said. "How long a wait do I have?"

She put a finger to her lips. I shut up. She picked up a phone. "Brenda, I reserved a table for one—Detective Lomax. Yes, he just strolled in. Come and get him."

She waved me through the door to the inner sanctum, and I didn't look back, but I'm sure all eight of the people in the waiting room were thinking, *Who the hell is he?*

Brenda, Doug Heller's senior nurse, met me on the other side. "Hey, Mike, you bolted out of here in a big hurry last week," she said.

"It's all part of the glamour of being a cop. This way I get to live in dread of a prostate exam yet a second time."

She led me into an exam room, took my BP and my pulse, and handed me a gown. "Suit up," she said. "Dr. Heller will be right in."

I stripped down, hung up my clothes, set my gun on the counter next to a container of cotton balls, and put on a pale blue, one-size-fits-nobody hospital gown with the wide slit down the back.

There was a knock on the door, and Doug Heller walked in.

"Oh, hi," I said, struggling to tie the gown in the back. "I was just trying on prom dresses. Do you have anything in a pink taffeta?"

Doug and I have been friends for twenty years, so we start every session with the usual *how's your family* stuff, or at the very least, some guy banter.

Not this time. "So, Mike," he said, skipping the foreplay, "how are you feeling?"

"Fine."

"Fine is not a medical term. You tired? Run down?"

"Overworked. Does that count?"

"Hop on the table."

I did as told, and he put his fingers on my neck and started pressing. "How about dizzy spells? Shortness of breath?"

"None of the above. What's going on?"

"I got your blood results from last week, and your white blood count is a little off. That's why I called you back."

"I thought it was because I bailed on the prostate exam."

"You're forty-three years old. I could have easily let it slide till your next physical," he said. "But this can't wait."

"What is it?"

"Probably nothing, but I'm going to take some more blood and run it through the lab again. Lie down."

I stretched out, and he began poking my belly.

"What do you mean my white blood count is a little off?" I said.

"Out of range. Nothing to worry about, but it's worth looking at again."

"What if I get the same bad numbers on the next blood test?" I said. "Do you have a guess what it could be?"

"Mike, I don't guess," he said, still stabbing his finger into my gut. "If you want guesswork, go to the Internet and Google the word *health*. You'll have millions of choices. Don't make yourself crazy. If the blood work doesn't change, I'll run a few tests. And the best news is they're free—all paid for by the Los Angeles Police Department. Have you used any steroids recently?"

"Jesus, Doug."

"Your lymph nodes are good, but your spleen is enlarged. Sit up, and I'll send Brenda back to draw some blood."

"So no prostate exam?"

"Almost forgot. Like I said, I wouldn't have called you back for it, but now that you're here and dressed for the occasion, let's get it done."

He reached over to the counter, took a latex glove out of a dispenser, and popped the cap off a tube of KY jelly.

"I hate this," I said, getting on my knees and lowering my shoulders to the table.

"It's not exactly April in Paris for me either, sweetheart."

My ass was up in the air when I heard the first gunshot. Instinct kicked in, and I jumped off the table.

"Holy shit," Doug said. "Was that a gunshot?"

"Yes, get down on the floor and stay there. If you've got a cell in your pocket, call 911."

I dove for the counter and had my hand on my Glock when the second shot rang out. Shotgun blast. And judging from the sound, the shooter was close by, but not in the next room. Doug's office was one of dozens in the San Vicente Medical Arts Building. I had no idea which one the shots came from.

I opened the exam room door and peered out. Patients and nurses alike were screaming and running toward the waiting room. "LAPD," I yelled. "Get back to your rooms. They're safer. Do it. Now. Now."

A third blast rang out. I could tell by the spacing that it was a pump-action shotgun. My Glock in front of me, and my bare ass hanging out behind me, I ran through the waiting room and headed toward the sound.

CHAPTER 2

I STEPPED INTO the communal hall. There were six other doctors' offices on that floor, and the door to every one of them was open. People were stampeding in my direction. Four-alarm panic. Whatever they were trying to get away from, I headed toward.

I can think of five other times in my career when I've had to run into a terrified crowd with my gun drawn. Three of those times I was in uniform, and twice in plain clothes with my badge on a chain around my neck. People were always relieved to see me, and the looks on their faces said it all. *Thank God—here comes the cavalry.*

Not this time. This time the reactions were more like, *oh shit—crazy man with a gun*. People either froze in their tracks, screamed, or both. Clearly, I'd have been a much more welcome sight if I had been wearing pants.

"LAPD. Get out, get out," I yelled, hoping that none of them were brave enough to try to tackle me.

I advanced down the hallway, barely looking at faces, just scanning the crowd for a weapon.

And then I saw him step through the center door at the far end of the corridor—white, middle-aged, balding, rimless glasses—hardly menacing, except for the Mossberg Pump-Action shotgun in his right hand.

"LAPD. Drop the gun," I bellowed.

He looked at me, dazed.

"LAPD," I shouted even louder. "Drop the gun. Now."

The gunman spooked, darted back into the office, and slammed the door behind him. I kicked it open, rolling to the floor as I came through the doorway.

Patients were huddled in corners, looking for protection behind fashionable teak side chairs that wouldn't protect them from a stiff kick, much less a 12-gauge shotgun blast.

"LAPD," I announced, jumping to my feet and looking in every direction.

A big beefy man closest to the door was acting as a human shield, his arms and body covering the woman beneath him. "In there," he said in a loud whisper, pointing toward an inside door.

I edged against the wall. All my training said, *wait for backup*. But my instincts said, *no time*. I dropped to a crouch and dove into the room.

The shooter was behind a desk in front of a window, the shotgun in his hand. But he wasn't pointing it at me. The barrel was tucked under his chin, and his right hand was extended all the way, his thumb on the trigger.

"Don't come any closer," he said.

I stopped cold. I'd had suicide prevention training, but I hadn't put it to use in years. Not only was I rusty, but I'm pretty sure the instructor never covered what to do if there's a dead man in a blood-soaked white coat lying on the floor only a few feet from the man whose life I was now obligated to save.

"I'm not moving," I said as slowly and calmly as I could. Meanwhile, my brain was racing back to the course material. *Introduce yourself. Give plenty of reassurance*.

"My name is Detective Mike Lomax," I said. "I'm with LAPD. I'm here to help."

"Too late, Mike."

"At least let's talk about it. What's your name?"

"Calvin Bernstein."

"Do you mind if I call you by your first name?" I asked.

"Cal. Call me Cal. Where the hell are your clothes?"

"Funny thing about that, Cal," I said. "I was at my doctor's office down the hall when— "

"I had no choice," he said. "I had to do it."

"Well that's definitely something we should sit down and talk about."

I could hear the sirens now. The building had been full of people. I could only imagine how many calls 911 logged since the first shot was fired. Cal heard them too.

"I'm sorry," he said, starting to sob. "I'm really sorry. I think you should leave now, Mike. You don't want to see this."

"Don't do it, Cal." I said. "We can work this out."

"Tell Janice I love her."

"I have a better idea, Cal. Why don't you pick up the phone on the desk, call Janice, and tell her yourself. I'm sure she'd much rather hear it from you."

"You're right. She would."

And then he pulled the trigger. Blood, bone and gray matter pelted the walls and the window behind him.

Nothing in my training prepared me for this. I'd only known Calvin Bernstein for the last two minutes of his life, but I took the loss personally. I stood there, stunned, shaking my head in disbelief. "Aww, Cal," I said. "I thought we were getting somewhere. I thought you were going to call Janice."

Cal didn't answer. If he could have, I'm sure it would have been something like, *It's not like I didn't warn you, Mike. I told you to leave. I told you that you don't want to see this.*

Whatever remained of Calvin Bernstein from the neck down had toppled to the floor. He was side by side with his victim, who was sprawled faceup on the rug, his frantic eyes staring blankly at the ceiling. I knelt down to get a closer look.

"Jesus," I said.

I knew him. His name was Kristian Kraus, and he was by far the best-known, most beloved fertility doctor in all of Los Angeles. Couples who desperately wanted to have a baby lined up at his door in the hopes that he could help them conceive one of Kristian's miracles.

Five years ago, my wife Joanie and I were one of those desperate couples. We tried every trick in the fertility handbook—stimulating ovulation, collecting sperm, screwing on a schedule. It cost a fortune, but nothing took.

And then, one day, about a year after we started, Dr. Kraus delivered the one thing we never expected—the news that Joanie had ovarian cancer.

Two years later, she died.

A voice came from behind me. It was young, female, and very shaky. "LAPD," she said. "Don't turn around. Just put the gun down nice and easy."

I didn't argue. I lowered my Glock to the floor. "I'm on the job, Officer," I said, not daring to turn around. "Detective Mike Lomax, Hollywood Division, Homicide Unit."

"I don't care who you are. Just stand up real slow, and put your hands in the air where I can see them."

I stood up. My hospital gown with the impossible-to-close slit down the back was embarrassing enough, but when I raised my arms high above my head, the gown hiked up, and the already immodest opening parted like the Red Sea.

I couldn't help myself. I started laughing.

"You think this is funny?" she said.

I looked down at the two bloody corpses on the floor. "Officer, from where I'm standing, nothing is funny, but I'll bet from your point of view, this little tableau has got to be a fucking laugh riot."

CHAPTER 3

AND THEN, A familiar voice. "Don't shoot him, Officer. He's one of the good guys."

"Are you sure?" the cop asked. "You can't see his face."

"Are you kidding?" the voice drawled. "I'd recognize that asshole anywhere. He's my partner."

"Officer," I said, "if Detective Biggs has finished making a bad situation worse, can I put my hands down and lower my skirt? I'd like to show a little respect for the dead."

"Trust me," Biggs said. "The living will be even more grateful."

I dropped my arms and turned around. The cop was young, blond, and pretty—not an easy trifecta for a woman trying to get ahead in a male-dominated department. But to her credit, she was the one holding the gun on me.

"Detective Lomax," she said, holstering her weapon. "I'm sorry. I've never seen anything like this. You had a gun. There were two dead bodies. I just—"

"You did fine. What's your name, Officer?'

"Barclay, sir. Dawn Barclay."

"This building is about to be inundated with cops, Barclay. Before they come running and gunning, get on the radio and tell them the situation is contained."

"Yes, sir."

"And tell them nobody leaves. Get IDs and hold everyone who hasn't already bolted until we find out what happened here."

"Yes, sir," she said and backed out of the office.

"So," Biggs said, "apart from the body count, how'd that prostate exam go for you?"

"I managed to get out of it again. Meanwhile, you were parked in front of the building. I figured you'd come running when the first shot was fired. Where the hell were you, anyway?"

"Victoria's Secret, shopping for peignoirs."

Terry Biggs wants to be a stand-up comic after he retires from the force. So he's always on. The problem is, he doesn't know when to turn it off.

"For God's sake, Terry, look at this mess. Lighten up on the jokes, will you?"

"I'm not kidding. You said you'd be about thirty minutes. Next week is my anniversary, so I drove over to the mall. I was trying to decide between a lace camisole and a satin baby doll when I heard 'shots fired' over the radio. At least give me some credit—I got here in time to save your sorry ass. Not to change the subject, but is that your gun on the floor?"

"Yeah."

"Don't bend over. I'll get it." He reached down, picked up the Glock, and smelled it. "You didn't fire your weapon," he said.

"No. The man on the left is Calvin Bernstein. At least that's what he told me just before he gave himself a Mossberg Pump-Action facelift. But first he unloaded three rounds into the other guy. Him I know. His name is Kristian Kraus. He was Joanie's doctor."

"Holy shit. He was Joanie's oncologist?"

"No. He's a fertility specialist. He tried to help us get pregnant, but in the end, all he managed to do was be the one to deliver the bad news."

"Fertility doc," Terry said, handing me my gun. "Doesn't seem like the kind of profession that gets you peppered with a

12-gauge. You think it was personal?"

"I don't know. The last thing he said to me before he killed himself was 'Tell Janice I love her.'"

"Then let's go find Janice," Terry said.

"I have a better idea," I said. "Why don't you walk over to Heller's office and find my clothes?"

"Me? I'm a goddamn detective. Send a uniform. Tell Barclay to go get your stuff."

"Terry, there is no way in hell that I'm asking a hot blond cop to bring me back my pants and underwear," I said. "You get them."

"I can't believe it," he said. "It took less than ten minutes for me to go from fondling Victoria's gauzy thongs to retrieving Mike Lomax's ragtag skivvies."

He started to leave, stopped, and turned around. "Y'know, as long as you're dressed for it," he said, grinning, "are you sure you don't want to toddle on across the hall and get that pesky prostate exam over and done with?"

"Thanks, but I'll pass," I said. "And if you see a guy wearing a white coat and a latex glove with a glob full of K-Y jelly on one finger, tell him to—oh, hell, you'll think of something—you're the comedian."

CHAPTER 4

JESSICA KEATING KNELT over the body of Kristian Kraus and shook her head. "Three shotgun blasts to the chest. Talk about overkill."

"Don't judge our shooter too harshly," Terry said. "It's still early in the investigation, but I think we've established that Mr. Bernstein was not exactly a professional."

Officer Barclay returned. "Nobody else was hurt," she reported, "although I'm sure several of the people I interviewed will be upping their Xanax intake for the next few days. Security cameras have the shooter's Volvo pulling into the parking lot at 1:14 p.m. He sat behind the wheel for eighteen minutes, finally got out, removed a four-foot-long canvas case from the trunk, and entered the building. Three minutes later, all hell broke loose."

"Any witnesses?" Terry asked.

"A long list, most of whom described a crazy man with a gun running down the hall half-naked, but the doctor's receptionist had a face-to-face with the shooter. Her name's Michele Melvin. She's waiting for you at the front desk."

I knew Michele. She'd worked for Kraus when Joanie was a patient, and despite the fact that she'd met thousands of infertile couples since then, she recognized me immediately.

"Detective Lomax," she said, offering me her hand. "I'm so sorry about your wife."

"You knew?"

"Dr. Kraus told me. He was very upset."

I nodded. My pants and my dignity had been restored, but I was still shaky after first staring down the barrel of a Mossberg, and then watching helplessly as Cal Bernstein blew his brains out. Bringing up my dead wife didn't help calm me down. "Can you tell us what happened?" I said.

"The man—the one who shot Dr. Kraus—came in. He was walking fast. He gets to my window and says, 'I'm meeting my wife, but I desperately need a bathroom before I sign in.' He's squirming all around like you do when you have to pee real bad, so I buzzed him in."

She closed her eyes and put her hand to her forehead. Cops see it all the time—an eyewitness reliving a moment of sheer horror that would stay with her for the rest of her life. We waited.

"And then I heard him yell Dr. Kraus's name," she said, opening her eyes. "Only it was more of a question, like he wanted to make sure he was talking to the right person. Then I heard the first shot, and I went on automatic pilot."

She looked at me and Terry to make sure we understood. We did, but we let her elaborate.

"I grew up in East LA. You hear gunfire; you take cover. You try to run, and you could wind up running into a bullet. I dove under the desk and prayed until I heard someone say, 'LAPD. Drop the gun.' That was you, wasn't it?"

I nodded.

She smiled. "You're the answer to my prayers."

"Did you know the man who shot him?" Terry asked.

"Never saw him before, but we get new patients all the time. It's the nature of the practice."

"His name is Calvin Bernstein. See if he's in your records."

She hesitated.

"What's the matter?" Terry said.

"Dr. Kraus is big on patient confidentiality, but I guess I'm allowed to break the HIPAA laws if my boss gets gunned down."

She searched her computer. "We've got six Bernsteins—no Calvins."

"Try Janice Bernstein," I said.

She went back to the computer. "Sorry. And nobody named Bernstein had an appointment today."

"Can you think of any reason anybody would want to kill Dr. Kraus?" I asked.

"No. You knew him, Mike. He dedicated his life to trying to give couples the one thing they wanted most in life." She pointed to a wall in the waiting room that was covered from floor to ceiling with baby pictures. "And even when they didn't conceive, he still gave them hope. People loved him."

"Somebody didn't," Terry said. "What can you tell us about his personal life?"

"Married, two kids in college."

"I'm looking for something a little more personal."

"You mean did he screw around? My last job, the doc had an affair. You can't keep that on the down low from the woman who answers your phone and opens your mail. But not Dr. Kraus. He was a good man."

"I'm sure he was," Terry said, "and we're very sorry for your loss."

She looked away. "Stupid, stupid, stupid," she said, pounding her desk with the flat of her fist. "I should never have buzzed him in."

"Michele," I said, "he came here to shoot Dr. Kraus. If you got in his way, he'd have shot you too."

She nodded. She knew I was right. It's just another one of those things you learn growing up on the streets of East LA.

CHAPTER 5

"YOU READY TO go?" Terry asked when we'd finished talking to Michele.

"Almost," I said. "I've just got to make a quick stop at Doug Heller's office."

"Good idea. He probably can tell us a few things about the victim. I'll go with you, partner."

"Nice try," I said, "but I can handle this on my own... partner."

Terry shrugged and headed for the car, and I walked back down the same hallway I raced through an hour ago. Doug's waiting room was empty, but Nadine was still at the front desk.

She looked up at me, the radiant smile gone, her face drawn in pain. "Mike," she said, "I wasn't sure you'd come back. Dr. Heller is in his office."

Doug was sitting at his desk. When it comes to death, especially something as violent and senseless as the murder of Kristian Kraus, doctors are no different from the rest of us. Doug was shaken to the core.

I sat down across from him. "Was he a friend?" I asked.

"More of a colleague, but one I liked. Hell, everybody liked him. Most docs deal with pain and suffering. If we're any good, we can make you feel better. Kris helped people make babies."

"Can you think of any reason why anyone would want to kill him?" I asked for the second time in the space of a few minutes.

He shook his head. "I've been sitting here trying to come up with an answer, and the only thing I can come up with is that maybe the killer got the wrong doctor."

"He asked for Dr. Kraus by name before he shot him."

"Why, Mike, why?"

"I don't know, but I'm going to find out. I've got a long day ahead of me. I'm going to ask for a rain check on that prostate exam."

He smiled. "No problem," he said. "Especially now that I realize it's not your prostate that's going to kill you. You're more likely to die in a shootout at your doctor's office."

"Thanks." I stood up.

"Not so fast," he said. "I still want Brenda to draw some blood before you go."

"You mind telling me why?"

"I will, but as your primary physician, there's something I have to say first. Next time you hear gunshots, don't go running towards them."

"Sorry, Doc, but that's my job."

"And that, Detective Lomax, is exactly why I'm running these blood tests. Now if you don't tell me how to do my job, I won't tell you how to do yours."

Ten minutes later, I was back in the car with Terry.

It was unseasonably warm for the middle of October, and I had made the mistake of not wearing my jacket.

"What's going on?" he said, pointing to the telltale Band-Aid taped over the vein in my left arm.

"I don't want to talk about it," I said. "With anybody. So don't say anything to Diana about driving me to Doug's office."

"You never told her you were going back for a follow-up?"

"No."

"Why?"

"Because she'd start worrying, and there's nothing to worry about."

"Well, you better tell her soon, because it's going to be all over the news that LAPD Detective Mike Lomax was in the doctor's office with his ass hanging out when the shooting went down."

He was right. I had to talk to Diana. But first Terry and I had to break the news to two women that they were now widows.

CHAPTER 6

BY THE TIME we arrived at Kristian Kraus's Mediterranean villa in Hollywood Hills, the street was crowded with TV news vans, camera crews, and reporters, all in search of juicy new details to feed a homicide-hungry public.

A maid let us in, walked us through the house and then out the back door. We followed a red brick path through a garden until we got to a small white bungalow.

"It's Mrs. Kraus's studio," the maid said. "She came back here to get as far away from the TV people as possible."

Nina Kraus opened the door and invited us in. She was in her mid-forties, wearing paint-spattered jeans and a man's shirt, with her blond curly hair tied up in a pink bandana. Her face was California tan, but her blue eyes were red from crying. The walls were covered with an eclectic mix of landscapes, portraits, and still lifes.

Terry and I extended our condolences and apologized for not getting to the house before the press arrived.

That set her off. "One of those bastards rang my doorbell," she said. "That's how I found out. He asked me how I felt about my husband being murdered. I thought it was some kind of a joke. But then another TV truck drove up. They're vultures."

She took a moment to regain her composure. "Who killed him?" she asked.

I gave her Calvin Bernstein's name.

"Was he a patient?"

"Michelle said she'd never seen him before. His name wasn't in her files."

"Then why? Why did he want to kill Kris?"

"We were hoping you could tell us," I said.

She shook her head.

"Did your husband have any enemies?"

Another head shake.

"Did he get any threats? Any ominous phone calls or texts?"

She didn't respond, and I remembered how I had clammed up just a few hours ago when Doug was bombarding me with stupid questions about dizzy spells, shortness of breath, or steroids.

"We have the killer," I said. "But we don't have a motive. Anything you can tell us about your husband might help us."

"Last year he got more than seven hundred Christmas cards," she said. "That's how much people loved him. Couples came to him, desperate, praying for a miracle, and for so many of them, Kris was the answer to their prayers."

I stood there unable to ask the next question. Joanie and I had been one of those couples. Only we didn't get what we came for.

Terry stepped in. "Mrs. Kraus, I'm sure your husband was a brilliant doctor, but not everyone can have a baby. Did any of them blame him?"

"I know what you're thinking, but no. Oh, sure, some of them were disappointed, but everyone knew that Kris tried his best. What they didn't know..." She stopped as the thought washed over her. "What they didn't know was how devastated he was when he couldn't help them get what they wanted most."

She started to sob. Fresh tears rolled down her cheeks, and she wiped her eyes with the sleeve of her shirt. It must have belonged to her husband, because the moment it touched her face, she made the connection, turned away from us, and wept uncontrollably into the frayed blue fabric.

Terry and I stood there, silent witnesses to her grief. We'd seen it hundreds of times before, and for me it is always the galvanizing moment when my commitment is no longer to the dead body inside the chalk outline. It's to the living. It's when my Inner Cop pledges to find the killer and bring him to justice.

But this time was different. I'd met the killer. We'd talked. "Tell Janice I love her," he'd said. Then Calvin Bernstein had provided his own justice.

His suicide may have gotten him off the hook, but not me or my partner. It just changed the nature of what Terry and I had to do for Nina Kraus—make sense of a totally senseless act.

CHAPTER 7

CAMERAS CLICKED, AND reporters shoved microphones in our faces as soon as Terry and I stepped out of the house and onto Kraus's front lawn.

We learned long ago that saying "no comment" is a waste of breath. It only encourages the news hounds to bark out their questions even louder, so we pushed our way through the crowd without saying a word.

"Do you agree with Mrs. Kraus?" Terry asked once we were back in the car.

"That the press are vultures?" I said.

"That's a given, but that's not the question. I'm talking about the doc. She made it sound like win or lose in the baby lottery, everyone thought he was a saint. You knew him. Do you feel that way?"

"Look, if you're asking did I send him Christmas cards, no. Besides, I'll bet most of those have pictures of happy families with healthy kids on them. We weren't that lucky."

"Sorry, Mike. I didn't mean to make you dredge this up."

"That's all right. The dredging started the second I saw Kraus lying in a pool of blood on his office floor," I said, letting my mind drift back to a moment in time that will live with me forever.

Kraus's office had been crowded that day. It was par for the course. He was always running late. But this time, as soon as we signed in, a nurse took us straight to an exam room. Two minutes later, Kraus walked in, sat down across from us, took Joanie's hand, and gave her the bad news. It's not easy to tell a woman who's there to get pregnant that she has to have her ovaries removed, but I doubt if anyone could have handled it better.

"I think Nina Kraus got it right," I said. "The man was dedicated to helping couples realize their dream. I met a lot of patients sitting around in that waiting room, and I never met anyone who didn't like him."

"Calvin Bernstein didn't."

"Bernstein didn't even know him. You heard what Michelle said. He had to double-check to make sure he was talking to Kraus before he—shit," I said, smacking my hand on the dashboard.

"What?"

"I've been looking at this whole thing ass backwards."

We were on a winding street in the Hills, and Terry pulled the car to the side of the road and stopped. "Talk to me."

"I keep running these scenarios through my head—what could Kraus have done that would make Bernstein want to kill him? It couldn't have been any worse than what happened to me and Joanie, and then it dawned on me—I've been thinking like a patient. Bernstein wasn't. Which means he wasn't there for revenge. I know this is coming out of left field, but maybe he was there because he had a job to do—kill Kraus. Think about it, Terry—who kills someone that they have no connection to?"

"You're saying Bernstein was a hit man?"

I almost laughed. "*Hit man* is way too generous. A professional contract killer has two goals. Pop the target and get away clean. Not this guy. First he decides that the best place to kill Kraus is in a crowded office building in the middle of a busy day. Then he brings along a gun that would fit in better at a turkey shoot. He whacks his victim with one shot, but does he toss the gun and run like hell? No. He sticks around and fires two more blasts into a dead man.

"When I cornered him, the first thing he said was, 'I had no choice. I had to do it. I'm sorry.' That's about as far from a pro as you can get. So, no—I can't call Cal Bernstein a hit man. I think he was probably a desperate soul who got paid to do somebody else's dirty work, and then was so filled with remorse after he'd done it that he blew his brains out."

Terry turned in his seat and looked me straight in the eye.

"Go ahead," I said. "Tell me how dumb I sound."

"Actually," Terry said, "you sound like the smartest cop in this car. I had the same dumb idea about twenty minutes ago, but I didn't have the brains or the balls to tell you what I was thinking."

CHAPTER 8

THE BERNSTEINS LIVED in a small stucco house in a working-class neighborhood in Van Nuys. There was a ten-year-old Toyota Matrix in the driveway.

"She's home," Terry said, ringing the bell.

A petite woman came to the screen door. "Yes?"

"Mrs. Bernstein," I said, holding out my ID. "Detectives Lomax and Biggs from the Los Angeles Police Department."

She knew why we were there before I said another word.

"It's Cal, isn't it?" she said, sobbing as she opened the door. "He's dead, right?"

"Yes ma'am," I said. "We are very sorry for your loss."

"I knew it was coming," she said, her face streaked with tears, "but you're never ready."

"*You knew*?" I said.

Her head snapped up. "*Did I know my husband was dying of a brain tumor*? What kind of stupid question is that?" she said, her jaw clenched, her eyes drilling me with unbridled rage. "I don't need the police anymore. Just tell me where he is. I have to make arrangements."

"Ma'am," Terry said. "I think we better go inside and sit down. There's something we have to tell you."

I'd run Janice Bernstein's name through the computer before we got there, so I knew she was only fifty-two, but she looked ten years older. Her hair was limp and gray, her brown eyes sleep-deprived, and the stress lines on her face had been etched in long before we arrived.

Breaking the news about a death is always difficult, but telling a woman that her husband murdered a total stranger and then blew his head off with a shotgun was as heart-wrenching an experience as I had ever gone through. And then I capped it off with Cal's final words.

It took twenty minutes before she could pull herself together and answer our questions coherently.

She had never heard of Kristian Kraus.

"Cal liked his doctors. Was he a brain surgeon? An oncologist?" she asked, trying to connect at least some of the dots.

"He was a fertility doctor," I said.

A faint smile. "Cal and I never had a problem in that department. We have two grown children, and then we called it quits. I don't think we even knew a—oh, my God, I just saw something about this on TV. They didn't have any details yet. Cal did that?"

"I'm afraid so, ma'am."

Another crying jag.

She had no idea why her husband would kill the doctor, but she could understand why he'd kill himself.

"Cal had an inoperable brain tumor," she said. "He'd been fighting it with radiation for six months, but it was a losing battle. Once he knew the clock was running out, he said he might have to bypass the end game. The last few weeks can be devastating. Severe pain, seizures, complete loss of body functions—there's a long ugly list, and he told me not to think less of him if he took the easy way out. I thought he might kill himself, but with pills—with me by his side, holding his hand. Death with dignity—it's what they taught him at LWD."

"LWD?" I repeated.

"Living With Dying. It's a support group like AA, only these people aren't in recovery. They have terminal illnesses, but they want to make the most out of the time they have left, and then hopefully..." She squeezed her eyes shut and clenched her hands. "And hopefully leave the world a better place than it was when they came into it."

"How old was your husband?" Terry asked.

"Fifty-four."

"Where did he work?"

"He was a manager at Sports Authority, but he stopped working a few weeks after he was diagnosed."

"Did he have medical coverage?"

"Not enough, but it didn't matter. He knew he was dying. No doctor could have saved him."

"Life insurance?"

She shook her head. "No. He's dead. Why is this important?"

"Mrs. Bernstein," Terry said, "your husband shot a man in cold blood. My partner and I just spoke to his widow. She wants to know why, and so do we."

Her face turned angry again. "And because Cal didn't have life insurance, you think he did it for money?"

"We have to consider it."

"You didn't know my husband," she said. "If you did, you'd consider this. He had a tumor the size of a tennis ball pressing on his frontal lobe. That would make anyone do crazy things. I'm sorry for the other woman's loss, but Cal would never hurt anyone—especially not for money. Please tell her that he was a wonderful human being, and that everybody who knew him loved him."

Word for word it was the same thing the victim's wife had said about her husband.

We left Janice Bernstein the same way we left Nina Kraus. In tears.

CHAPTER 9

TERRY AND I drove back to the station. Eileen Mulvey at the front desk flagged us down as soon as we walked through the door. "Guess who's looking for you two guys," she said.

"If it's anyone but Scarlett Johansson, I don't want to know," Terry said.

"You're in luck. It *is* Scarlett. She waiting for you in Kilcullen's office."

"Tell her I'm sorry to disappoint her, Officer Mulvey, but I'm trying to steer clear of the boss until he gives up on that caveman diet and goes back to being the same old pain in the ass that he's always been."

"Don't count on it, Biggs. He's digging in his heels," Mulvey said. "This morning he had maintenance move the candy machine out of the break room. He replaced it with a ten-point list on how sugar can kill you."

"Are you serious? I put my life on the line every day chasing gangbangers, dope dealers, mob rats, and homicidal maniacs, and that overweight caveman is afraid I'm going to be taken out by a bag of Skittles?"

"I'm starting to get the sense that you really want to chat with Lieutenant Caveman as much as he wants to talk to you," Mulvey said, picking up the phone. "Should I call and tell him you're back, or would you rather just go straight to his office?"

"I don't know," Terry said. "What would make you more of an ass kisser?"

"Definitely calling," she said, dialing. "Hello, Lieutenant. Detectives Lomax and Biggs are back. Yes sir, I'll tell them." She hung up.

"What did he say?" Biggs asked.

"He said it's about bleeping time those two assholes showed up."

Terry and I headed down the hall. "Listen," I said, "I've had a difficult day. Don't make it worse by poking the bear."

"But the bear took my candy machine."

"Busting his balls won't bring your Skittles back."

"You never know till you try," Terry said as we walked into the boss's office.

Brendan Kilcullen is a smart cop and a decorated detective, but he'll never win a prize for his leadership skills. He has the patience of a six-year-old kid on Christmas morning, and about as much tact as a brick flying through a plate glass window.

He was at his desk munching a carrot stick. There were half a dozen plastic bags on the desktop filled with the raw vegetables, fruits, and nuts allowed on the Paleo diet. "What the hell is going on with this dead doctor?" he bellowed, bits of orange vegetation flying from his mouth.

"All we know is that the shooter was Joe Average," I said. "Calvin Bernstein, family man, worked at Sports Authority, no criminal record, no connection to Kraus."

"What about drugs?" Kilcullen said. "A lot of these docs go through prescription pads the way I go through toilet paper. He wouldn't be the first doc who was killed because he cut off some hophead's supply of Oxy."

"Dead end, Loo," I said. "Kraus didn't write scripts for street drugs. He got the big bucks for stimulating ovaries to produce eggs. Biggs and I are coming around to the thought that Bernstein was a hired gun."

"But not exactly one who will ever get elected to the Hit Man's Hall of Fame," Terry said. "He was so clueless that he asked the receptionist to point the victim out."

"Point the victim...? Son of a bitch. Are you telling me that somebody wanted to whack this doc, so they hired some idiot who worked in a sporting goods store?" he said, popping a few cashews in with the carrots. "What'd they do—run an ad on Craigslist? Hit Man Wanted. No Experience Necessary."

"We spoke to Bernstein's widow," I said. "He had cancer. He only had a few weeks left to live, and he had no life insurance."

"So he needs a quick payday, and he offs a guy so Mama has some money after he's gone," Kilcullen said.

"That's what we're thinking."

"Are you also thinking about what kind of mastermind would hire a rank amateur to bump off a big-shot doctor?"

"That's what we're working on," I said.

"Oh, that's sweet. I can tell the mayor that *we're working on it*."

"The mayor?" Terry said. "Doesn't he have ribbons to cut and palms to be greased? LAPD has over two hundred homicides a year. Why are we reporting to him on this one?"

"*We*? There's no *we*, Biggs. I'm the one who's always got half of City Hall up his ass." He swiveled his computer so we could look at the monitor. "The mayor sent me this," he said, clicking on a file.

A picture opened up on the screen. A smiling family of five.

"That's the mayor's daughter, her husband, and their three kids," Kilcullen said. "Triplets."

Terry frowned. "And I'm guessing the three little darlings were conceived in a petri dish."

"The mayor said it more elegantly. I believe his exact words were, 'My grandchildren were gifts from God and a brilliant and dedicated reproductive endocrinologist.'"

"Kristian Kraus," Terry said.

"This was not a random homicide," Kilcullen said, pulling a limp piece of celery out of a bag, and then putting it back. "This was Murder One. The mayor and his entire family are devastated. They know who pulled the trigger, but they don't understand why. They need answers, and so do I. You get it now, Biggs?"

Terry grunted.

"Anything else, detectives?"

"One thing," I said. "Joanie and I were patients of Dr. Kraus. He's the one who diagnosed her with ovarian cancer. Since this case is now up to its ears in politics, I want to make sure you don't think it's a conflict of interest."

"Did Kraus do anything wrong? Did you have a beef with him?"

"No. He was a good doctor. Plus I haven't had contact with him in about four years."

"No connection, no conflict," Kilcullen declared. "Now, how about you, Biggs? Anything on your troubled brain?"

"Yeah, but no, never mind. I'll figure it out on my own. You already have a full plate," he said, taking a sideways glance at the meager assortment of bagged edibles.

"Hey—whatever it is, it's my job, Biggs. Spit it out."

"As long as you really want to know," Terry said. "Somebody stole the candy machine out of the break room."

Kilcullen erupted. "Get out."

He didn't have to scream it twice. Terry was gone. The bear had been poked.

CHAPTER 10

TERRY AND I laid out a game plan for the morning, and fifteen minutes later I was driving down Highland headed for the freeway.

The drive to my house in Santa Monica is my decompression time. I try to turn off my mind and let go of the ugliness of the day. And this day was uglier than most. Dr. Kraus in a pool of blood, Cal Bernstein blowing his brains out, Doug Heller dodging my medical questions, and toughest of all, dredging up the loss of my wife.

Joanie's death was the lowest point in my life, and I only got through it because of the two most annoying men on the planet. My partner, Terry Biggs, and my father, Big Jim Lomax. No matter how hard I tried, they refused to let me wallow in self pity. Especially Big Jim. He'd suffered after my mother died, and he was determined to help spare me some of the pain.

Six months to the day after Joanie died, Big Jim and his new wife, Angel, invited me to dinner. They also invited Diana Trantanella—my age, my type, and recently widowed herself. It was a blatant ambush date, and I was pissed. But it's hard to stay mad when you're falling in love. Now, almost two years later, I can't think of what my life would be without Diana.

I was almost on the verge of asking her to marry me when our lives got interrupted. Diana's friend Carly Tan asked us to take care of her daughter Sophie so Carly could fly home to China to be with her dying mother. It was a no-brainer. The old woman was on life support, so we knew we'd only be babysitting for a week—two at the most.

That was five months ago. Since then, Sophie Tan had become part of the fabric of our lives. She's a bright, bubbly, fun-loving eight-year-old with a passion for writing, and the fertile imagination to produce stories that can be so insightful that her teacher once called me and Diana in and asked us to stop helping her write them.

"We're not," Diana told the teacher. "It's all her."

"My God," the teacher said. "What is she doing in the third grade?"

"Trying to stay normal," I said.

Sophie was the daughter every parent would wish for, and I adored coming home to her. Unfortunately, she was only a loaner kid. One of these days, I knew we'd have to give her back.

When I got home that evening, Diana greeted me with the three words that signaled that the day I was dreading had finally arrived.

"Grandma Xiaoling died."

"When is Carly coming back?"

"Thursday."

It was Tuesday.

"Where's Sophie?" I asked.

"I have a question for you first," Diana said. "What were you doing at Dr. Heller's office?"

"I guess you caught the news," I said.

"You mean the story about the hero cop who ran through the halls in a hospital gown to confront a lunatic who killed a beloved fertility doctor?"

"Cal Bernstein wasn't a lunatic."

"Well, it sounds like the cop in the hospital gown is," she said. "Tell me about him."

"If you're lucky, you'll get to sleep with him tonight. And if you ask real nice, he may just let you sneak a little peek under the gown."

"Damn it, Mike, it's not funny. You had your physical last week. Why were you back in the doctor's office?"

"He didn't get to the prostate exam the last time around, plus he wanted some more blood."

"Did he say why?"

"He said there's nothing to worry about."

"Did he say you're okay?"

"Better than okay. He said I'm indestructible."

Diana wrapped her arms around me and kissed me.

"Now where's Sophie?" I said.

"In her room. She's waiting for you."

I went upstairs. Sophie was at her computer. "What are you doing?" I said.

"Writing a story."

"About what?"

"Death," she said, looking up from the keyboard.

"I'm sorry about Grandma Xiaoling."

"It's okay. We all die, Mike. The best thing to do is have as much fun with your life while you can. That's what I'm writing about."

"Is it too late for me to remind you that you're eight years old, and most girls your age are writing about unicorns and rainbows?"

"Most people would rather read a story about someone dying than about a stupid horse with a horn sticking out of its head."

"Point taken," I said. "So who's the hero of your little drama?"

"A girl whose grandmother dies."

"You mean you?"

"No. It's a fictional girl."

"And how does this fictional girl feel?"

"She's sad. But she understands. Her grandmother had a good

life, and now it was her time to go."

"How about the real girl? How do you feel about your grandmother dying?"

"Sad. Then happy because my mom is finally coming home. Then sad again because I'm going to miss you and Diana."

"We'll miss you too," I said. "But we're still going to see you."

"It won't be the same, Mike."

Damn right it wouldn't. The kid was wise beyond her years.

"We should commemorate the occasion," I said. "Give you a big sendoff and your mom a big welcome home."

Her eyes lit up, and she clasped her hands together. "You mean a party?"

"Sure. Why not?"

"Could we do it at Big Jim's house?"

"I don't know," I said. "Then we'd have to invite Big Jim."

That got a big giggle.

"We may as well invite him," I said. "You know my father. He's going to show up anyway."

"And Frankie. We definitely need Frankie. And Izzy."

"You want them with or without their Big Ugly Food Truck?"

"Duh-uh," she said. "It's a party. We've got to eat."

"Gotcha. We'll invite Frankie and Izzy and tell them that they're in charge of feeding us. Make a list of everything you want, and we'll get it done."

"Awesome. I'll do it as soon as I finish my story."

"It shouldn't take you long," I said. "I mean what does a kid your age know about death?"

She looked up and gave me a gap-toothed smile. "I know a lot more about death than I do about unicorns."

"Me too, kiddo," I said, kissing the top of her head. "Me too."

CHAPTER 11

DIANA, SOPHIE, AND I have our morning routine down to a science. The coffee starts brewing at 5:45, alarm clocks go off at 6:30, we sit down for breakfast at 7:00, and we're out the door at exactly 7:20. Diana drives to Valley General Hospital where she's a pediatric oncology nurse. I head to the Hollywood station, dropping Sophie off at Bradfield—a private school on West Olympic.

"I'm going to miss being your chauffeur every morning," I said, opening the back door for Sophie and making sure she was buckled up. "After five months, we're like a finely tuned, well-oiled machine."

"We're more like the Rockettes," Sophie said, rewriting me as usual.

"What does a kid from LA know about a bunch of dancers in New York?"

"Tons," she giggled. "I Googled them."

"You know, if I were your father instead of just your congenial host and proprietor of the Hotel Lomax, I wouldn't let you be Googling your way around the Internet," I said. "Not everything on the information highway is PG, kiddo."

"I know, but my mother thinks there's a lot I can learn from the kid-friendly websites. Plus, she trusts me to be careful on highways—the 405, the 101, the Internet." She giggled again.

Sophie is her own best audience, but I was quickly becoming a close second.

"What ever possessed you to Google the Rockettes anyway?" I asked.

"It was an accident. You know how Google always tries to figure out what you're looking for before you even finish putting in the whole word. I was typing *rocketry* but Google guessed the *Rockettes*, so I checked them out."

"And?"

"Those ladies are like a finely tuned, well-oiled machine."

Big giggles. From both of us.

"What are you and Terry doing today?" she asked as I took the ramp onto the 10.

"Oh, the usual. Round up some bad guys, lock them up, throw away the key."

"Oh, give me a break, man," she said. "What are you *really* doing?"

As much as I didn't want my conversation with an eight-year-old to come back around to death again, I've always been straight with her, so I told her the truth. "We're starting out at the morgue."

"Cool. One of these days, can I go to the morgue with you?"

I took a look at her in the rearview mirror to see if she was still joking around. She wasn't.

"You know," she said hopefully. "Like Take Your Daughter To Work Day."

"Oh, in that case," I said, "absolutely."

That threw her. "Really? When can we go?"

"As soon as I find a kid-friendly morgue that your mom will approve of. Otherwise, you can wait till you're in medical school."

"I don't want to be a doctor. I want to be a detective like you."

"Okay, then wait till you're in detective school."

"Not fair," she said, sticking her tongue out and contorting her face into an exaggerated scowl—a clear message that she thought my decision to spare her a naked cadaver being sliced open from stem to stern was the ultimate in bad surrogate parenting.

"I'm sorry to dash your dreams, kiddo," I said, "but can we change the subject to something more pleasant? Something without dead people."

"Okay, how about you take me to a shooting range?"

My cell rang.

"Put it on speaker," the wise-ass kid said.

"In your dreams," I told her.

I'd learned the hard way that hitting the Bluetooth button on the steering column and broadcasting my calls—especially the ones from my foul-mouthed, scatological boss Brendan Kilcullen—was a sure-fire way to expand Sophie's vocabulary.

I plugged in my ear buds and took the call.

"Mike, it's Doug Heller. I got your blood test back."

"And?"

"And your white blood count went from 18,000 to 22,000."

"I'm in the car with Sophie," I said.

"So you can't ask me any probing questions," he said.

"Correct."

"Good, because I wouldn't have any intelligent answers. All I can tell you is that the upper limit of normal is 10,000, and your numbers are heading in the wrong direction. I want you to see a friend of mine, Herand Abordo. He's a hematologist."

"Fine," I said.

"*Fine*? How about, 'What's Dr. Abordo's phone number, Doug, because this sounds like something I shouldn't put off?'"

I laughed. "I'm kind of busy right now."

"That's what I figured, so I made an appointment for you. This afternoon at five. I'll text you his address. Have a nice day."

He hung up.

"Sure thing, Dad," I said into the dead phone. "I'll tell her."

"Was that Big Jim?" Sophie asked as soon as I pulled out my ear buds.

"Oh... were you listening to my phone call?"

"That's what detectives do," she said.

"Well, Detective Tan, Big Jim just called to say he's excited about the party. He wants to know who you're inviting."

She handed me a piece of paper. "I made a list last night."

I glanced at it. "No kids from your class?"

"No. It's a family thing, not a school thing."

"Big Jim has four acres, and so far it feels like a pretty small party. Why don't you invite some more people?"

"How many?" she said.

"As many as you want."

"Okay," she said, a gap-toothed imp grin spreading across her face. "How about the Rockettes?"

God, I loved this girl. I was going to miss her something fierce.

CHAPTER 12

THE LA COUNTY Morgue is the last place on earth I'd take Sophie to. It's definitely not kid-friendly and not particularly adult-friendly either. For starters, it's nothing like the morgues you see on TV. Those are so spacious and pristine, it's like the set designers are trying to make you feel like you could have your family picnic right there on the stainless steel autopsy table.

But that's make believe, and in real life, real death isn't pretty. The LA Morgue looks more like a Civil War battlefield after the carnage. There are bodies everywhere. Not tucked out of sight in gleaming steel drawers, but on gurneys scattered helter-skelter in the dank hallways—some of the corpses draped with sheets, some not-so-draped, all waiting to be processed, claimed, or stored indefinitely like so many old suitcases that have piled up in the Lost and Found department of a train station.

And trust me, nothing smells like luggage.

I pulled into the parking lot, took my last few breaths of fresh air, entered through the loading dock, and stopped at the admissions desk.

"Good morning, Mike," the tech behind the counter said. "Terry is in Autopsy Three with Doc Hand."

That made me smile. When you've watched as many autopsies as I have, it's only natural to have a favorite pathologist. For me and Terry, it was Eli Hand.

When I first met Eli, he introduced himself as a recovering rabbi. As a young man he went to rabbinical school, found a congregation, and after two years, realized he could no longer stand listening to other people's problems.

"I was like a shepherd who wakes up one morning and thinks, 'This job would be so much better if it weren't for all these needy sheep,'" he told me. "One a day, two a day—that I might have tolerated. But it was a steady stream of complainers. Like I was their shrink. At one point I told the president of the synagogue we should change our name to Temple Beth Oy, Do I Have A Problem."

So after two years of trying, Eli said farewell to his flock, went to medical school, and picked the one specialty that was a perfect match for his intellect and his temperament. Now in his seventies, he is the most respected pathologist on the morgue staff. "And," he adds proudly, "not one of my patients has ever complained."

I weaved my way past the recently departed and entered Autopsy Three. Eli, Terry, and the two homicide-suicide victims from yesterday were waiting for me.

"How's it going?" Terry said.

"Not so good. Sophie's grandmother died."

Eli looked up from the remains of Cal Bernstein. "So does that mean her mother is coming back from China?"

"Thursday," I said.

He said something softly in Hebrew.

"What are you mumbling?"

"*Baruch dayan emet*. Blessed Is the True Judge. If you've got the life event, I've got the blessing. It comes in handy in my line of work."

"Thanks. I'll tell Carly you said a prayer for her mother."

He shrugged his shoulders and gave me a hangdog look. "Mike, she was an old lady, and we all knew she was dying, so the prayer was only maybe ten percent for her. The other ninety percent was for you and Diana, because I know how you're going to feel about giving up Sophie."

"You're bumming me out, Doc. Let's talk about something more upbeat, like those two bodies you've been hunched over."

Eli stepped back from the table. "It didn't take much hunching. Dr. Kraus was shot three times, any one of which would have done the trick. Mr. Bernstein, as you saw for yourself, blew his brains out. The parts of his body that were still intact are riddled with cancer. He only had weeks to live himself. My part was easy. You boys have the tough job of figuring out a motive—that's what I'd like to know."

"You and the mayor of Los Angeles," Terry said. "Apparently Dr. Kraus is the miracle worker responsible for his three grandchildren."

"Just what every criminal investigator needs," Eli said. "A politician looking over your shoulder."

"We'll figure it out," Terry said.

"You're a mensch, Biggs," Eli said. "The department could use a few more like you and Mike."

"Would you mind repeating that? I've never heard it before, and I doubt if I'll ever hear it again."

"I mean it. I hate working with cops who either don't give a crap, or they sweep the loose ends under the rug so they can close a case."

"Are you talking about any cops in particular?" I said.

"You mean like those two assholes over in West LA, Detectives Rubsam and Apovian?" Eli said.

"Don't know them," Terry said. "What'd they do to piss off a rabbi?"

"I'll tell you all about it over a cup of coffee," Eli said. "You got ten minutes?"

Terry grinned. "Ten minutes? I know you, Eli. Are you sure that's all we're going to need?"

"For starters," Eli said. "Unless you want to help out a friend and get involved. Then it will take a little more time."

"Help out a friend?" Terry said. "Oy, now Eli has a problem."

Eli smiled, gave Terry the finger, and said something in Hebrew. I doubt if it was a blessing.

CHAPTER 13

WE FOLLOWED ELI upstairs to the employee lounge, where the plastic plaque on the door read Life Goes On. It was a spacious room with a bank of vending machines, a tidy little kitchenette, and half a dozen crisp white Formica tables, each one surrounded by a quartet of bright orange chairs.

The morning sun streamed through a wall of oversized windows. It was a total departure from the bleak Dickensian world we'd just left behind two floors below.

We each popped a single-serve K-Cup into the Keurig coffeemaker and sat down at a table furthest from the door.

"I had a body in here three weeks ago," Eli said, sprinkling a packet of Splenda into his Green Mountain Breakfast Blend, "male, Caucasian, forty–seven years old. His name was Wade Yancy. He had been at home, went out to walk his dog on a dark road, and got hit by a car.

"According to the accident report, the driver was sober. The victim, on the other hand, had tied one on. There was enough alcohol in his blood to convince me that Mr. Yancy was the primary cause of his own death. He landed on a neighbor's lawn about sixty feet from the point of impact, so no surprise that the autopsy showed multiple broken bones along with catastrophic internal bleeding."

"So far it sounds like another open-and-shut case," Terry said.

"And yet..."

Eli nodded, sat back, and looked at us over his coffee cup. He had our undivided attention. "And yet, Mr. Yancy died from blunt force trauma to the head."

"You said he sailed sixty feet. He must've conked his noggin when he landed."

"He hit the *back* of his head—the occipital bone—but it wasn't enough to cause death. However, he also had a grievous injury to the top of his head, which was not consistent with the rest of the accident. And since there was no indication that the top of his head ever came in contact with the ground, I concluded that he was struck with a blunt object which caved in part of his skull."

"So maybe Mr. Yancy wasn't the primary cause of his own death after all," Terry said.

"Now you're talking like a detective who wouldn't rule it a fatal traffic accident and waive any further investigation."

"Is this where Rubsam and Apovian come in?"

"They were assigned to do the follow-up. I called them, told them what I'd found, and sent them pictures of this mysterious head wound. I never heard back from them. A few days later, they filed a report saying no signs of foul play, and I had to release the body to Yancy's family. It annoyed the crap out of me, so on Sunday I decided to do what I always do when I'm trying to solve a problem."

"You went to temple and prayed," I said.

"No. I went to Hillcrest and played golf. Me, my wife, and another couple. We were on the seventh hole when it came to me. An epiphany."

"You finally realized that Jesus Christ is the Son of God," Terry said.

Eli chuckled. "That's an Epiphany with a capital *E*. Mine was a lowercase *e*."

"More like a hunch," Terry said.

"No. I'm not paid to have hunches. I had an educated medical opinion on what really killed Wade Yancy, and it wasn't a Prius."

He paused to sip his coffee. Rabbi/Doctor Hand was a master of dramatic effect.

"So what do you think killed him?" I asked.

"Bam!" he said, banging the flat of his fist against the table. "Someone clobbered him on the head with a golf club. Judging by the shape of the indentation, my best guess is a nine-iron. So I called Rubsam and Apovian and told them to get a warrant to search the driver's house and car for a set of clubs. If I'm right, I might be able to pick up some of Yancy's DNA from the murder weapon."

"You're calling it murder?" I said.

"Could I testify in court that it was murder beyond a reasonable doubt? No. The man was hit by three thousand pounds of steel travelling at forty miles an hour. The fact that he didn't die on impact was a miracle. His life force was gone. His organs were shutting down. But it looks to me like someone couldn't wait a few more minutes and decided to hurry the process along."

"And what did Rubsam and Apovian say?"

"They think I'm a crazy old man."

"It's hard to argue with that," Terry said. "But what was their official response?"

"'Not enough probable cause for a warrant.' I went ballistic. *Probable cause*? What the hell do they need—a Titleist logo imprinted on the victim's brain? They blew me off and told me the case is wrapped up."

"And what would you like us to do?"

"Unwrap it," Eli said. "If you don't mind another dead body on your plate, I'd appreciate it if you looked into this one."

"After all the nice things you said about me and Mike this morning, we'd look like total jerks if we turned you down," Terry said.

Eli shrugged. "That may have crossed my mind when I was buttering you up."

"It worked," Terry said. "We'll do it."

"Thank you. I'll get you Yancy's paperwork." He started to leave and then turned back. "One more favor," he said. "Mike, you're good with computers. Mine is acting up. Can you give it a quick look?"

"He's better at tech stuff than I am," I said, looking over at Terry.

"No, no, you do it," Terry said. "I still haven't bought Marilyn an anniversary present. Why don't I meet you back at the office in an hour?"

He left, and Eli and I started down the hall towards his office. "What's wrong with your computer?" I said.

"Not a damn thing, Mike. What's wrong with you?"

"Nothing."

"Then what the hell were you doing in Doug Heller's office yesterday?"

CHAPTER 14

I'D BEEN TOTALLY sandbagged, and the best I could come back with was, "Me? What are you talking about?"

"I may be a crazy old man, but I pay attention to details. You told me last week that you had your annual department physical. Then it turns out yesterday you were back there again. Under ordinary circumstances I would never have known, but when your name and rank are at the top of a murder/suicide file, the news is definitely going to cross my desk. So let me repeat the question—why were you back in Doug Heller's office yesterday if you passed the physical last week?"

"What happened to the crotchety old rabbi who gave up his congregation because he hated dealing with other people's problems?"

"Those people were whiners. This is different. You're not complaining. I'm meddling. Answer the question."

"I don't really have any answers. Doug didn't like my white blood cell count, so he called me in and helped himself to some more."

"And that's all he said?"

"I was trying to pry more information out of him when the bullets started flying, and I had to run down the hall and watch a man blow his head off. After that, I didn't really give a shit. I just let him draw some more blood, then Terry and I made *shiva* calls to the widows of the two guys you just cut open."

We got to Eli's office, and he shut the door behind us. "Did he tell you the white blood count number?"

"He called me this morning. I went from 18,000 to 22,000. As long as you're meddling, do you mind telling me what's the big deal?"

"Over ten thousand is a red flag. Twenty-two thousand is sinister. He's going to tell you to see a hematologist."

"He already did. I have an appointment at five o'clock with a Dr. Abordo."

"I know Herand Abordo. He's top drawer. He'll take some more blood and do a bone marrow biopsy."

"What's he looking for?"

"He's checking you for the Philadelphia chromosome. It's pathognomonic."

"Path… what?"

"Pathognomonic. It means characteristic of one particular disease. Sometimes your doc can run a test, and something will come up, but it can translate to any one of a dozen different conditions. The Philadelphia chromosome is different. If that shows up, then Heller will know exactly why your white blood cell count is out of whack."

"And what's that?"

"I already told you more than I should have. Why don't you wait for the results of the bone marrow biopsy?" He handed me a folder. "Here's the file on Wade Yancy."

I handed it back to him. "First things first, Eli. What does it mean if I have this Philadelphia chromosome?"

"Oy," he said, letting it trail off into a long sigh. "It would be an indicator that you have CML."

"You're making it sound harmless—like this episode of *Sesame Street* is brought to you by the letters *C*, *M*, and *L*. Give me the nasty medical terms that go along with them."

"He's checking you for Chronic Myeloid Leukemia."

I felt my knees buckle, and I sat down. "He thinks I have leukemia?"

"He doesn't *think* you have anything. He's trying to rule out CML. But even if you tested positive, it's not the kind of leukemia that means a death sentence. It can smolder on for years without presenting, and if you get symptoms, there are treatments."

"You're trying to make it sound like it's the fun, good leukemia that all the popular kids get, but I'm not buying it." I picked up Wade Yancy's file. "Tick tock. I guess I better get to this in a hurry."

"Cut the theatrics, Mike, and listen to me. You haven't been diagnosed with leukemia—good, bad, or otherwise—so do me a favor. Don't throw yourself off that bridge until you get to it."

"Do *me* a favor, Doc. Don't mention this to anybody—especially Terry."

"Understood. Just tell me one thing—how do you feel?"

"This little talk of ours has scared the shit out of me, but the truth is I feel great. Best I've felt in a long time."

"Good. Then don't worry," he told me.

What he didn't tell me was that feeling great didn't rule out Chronic Myeloid Leukemia.

CHAPTER 15

I DROVE BACK to the station, grateful for the alone time. I kept running the letters *CML* through my head, but mostly I focused on *L*. Leukemia.

There was only one cure. I hit the number-one button on my CD player, and kicked the volume up. I took a deep breath and smiled. It's hard to be bummed when George Harrison is singing "Here Comes The Sun." "What did Eli want?" Terry asked me as soon as I got back to the office. "And if you have any respect for me, please don't attempt to perpetuate that hocus-pocus about computer repair. I have a graduate degree from the Acme School of Bullshit Detection, so you have two choices. You can either tell me to go fuck myself, or you can tell me the truth."

I didn't hesitate. I told him the truth. All of it—which wasn't a lot.

"Does Diana know?"

"She knows I was at the doc's, but I played it down. No sense getting her crazy till some of the blanks get filled in."

He nodded. It wasn't judgmental. Just a nod.

"Thanks for telling me," he said. "Let me know if you need anything. Y'know—like time off. Or a kidney. Whatever."

We looked over the file on Wade Yancy. The accident report was textbook, and except for Eli's protestations, there was nothing to indicate foul play.

We put the phone on speaker, called the West LA Division, and asked for either Detective Apovian or Rubsam. We got Apovian, and as soon we told him what we wanted, he got his hackles up.

"What do you know about the victim?" he demanded. "Did Eli give you anything besides a list of broken bones and a bunch of medical gobbledygook?"

"It's a coroner's report," Terry said. "Medical gobbledygook is a requirement. Why don't you tell us what you know."

"Wade Yancy was a honcho at a drug company—Vice President of Brand Development, or some fancy title like that. Basically he was in marketing. The company makes the drugs, Yancy was in charge of peddling them. He made good money—more than enough to buy top-shelf liquor, and apparently he drank his fair share of it. He had a wife, two daughters, belonged to a church, and as far as we could tell, he had no enemies. Everybody liked him. Zero motive."

"What about life insurance?"

"His wife gets a lump sum equal to about three years of his salary," Apovian said. "From my experience, nobody kills the goose that's been laying the golden eggs."

"What can you tell us about the driver?" I said.

"His name is Bruce Bower. He's an accountant. He didn't know the victim, and there's no record the vic knew him. They lived a few miles apart, but it was like they were from two different planets. That night, Bower went out for ice cream with his old lady. The road was dark, Yancy was sloshed, he bent down to pick up some dog shit, and you don't have to be a detective to figure out the rest. Road karma. It happens about five thousand times a year across this great land of ours, and Los Angeles is proud to contribute our fair share of the body count."

"Eli thinks he got whacked on the head with a golf club," Terry said.

"So he said."

"Did you look for a set of clubs in Bower's house or his car?"

"Not yet," Apovian said. "My partner and I decided to wait for Search Without Probable Cause Day. Let me give you guys a reality check. Everything's a homicide with Eli, but as far as I can tell, the only connection between the driver and the victim was three thousand pounds of Japanese car. There's nothing in the accident report to suggest that we keep beating this dead horse.

"On the other hand, we have a thirty-two-year-old widow whose seventy-five-year-old husband *accidentally* drowned in his own pool, leaving behind a twenty-million-dollar estate; a pair of gangbangers who were standing on the wrong side of a drive-by; a liquor store owner who thought he could stop an armed robbery with a baseball bat; not to mention a shitload of paperwork from cases we already solved, but refuse to go away. So to answer your question, Detectives, no, we don't have the time to find out if Bruce Bower plays golf. If you do, you have our blessings to have at it."

He let out a long, loud exhale.

"Sorry," he said. "You caught me on a bad day. The captain put me and Rubsam on a double shift, and I slept on a cot at the station last night. I'm two hundred and forty-seven days away from pulling the pin, and I'm hoping my wife and kids will recognize me when I retire. I'm not usually this big a dick. For the record, I've never bagged a case because my plate was too full. I think Eli is wrong. Everything I see screams accident, but I'll have a uniform run the Yancy file over to you. We good?"

"We're good," I said, and we hung up.

"Eli is wrong about one thing," Terry said. "This guy's not an asshole. He's just another double-shift cop trying to work a triple-shift job."

CHAPTER 16

"APOVIAN CALLED IT," Terry said after we'd gone through the file on Wade Yancy. "There's nothing in here that looks like evidence of a crime."

"You think Eli got it wrong?"

Terry shrugged. "It's possible. It's also possible that Bruce Bower got away with murder, but we can't prove it, because we can't search his house, and if we showed up and started grilling him, the murder weapon—if there ever was one—would disappear faster than you can say 'Jimmy Hoffa.'"

"So what do we do?"

"We decide which one of us is going to tell Eli that there is no warrant in his future. I vote for you."

"Thank you for your support, Detective Biggs. And I in turn vote for you."

"What are you guys voting for?" It was Muller, our resident geek.

"We were just trying to decide which one of us should tell Kilcullen he's depriving the squad of three of our five most important food groups," Terry said.

"Do you believe that?" Muller said. "The man just unilaterally banned sugar."

"I don't know if I can function without my daily Skittles fix," Terry said. "And this is just the beginning. Who knows what he'll take away next—drugs, alcohol, Internet porn? What do you want, kid?"

"I'm here to tell you guys that your cop instincts are bordering on brilliant."

"Old news," Terry said. "You'll have to be more specific."

"I went through the LUDs on Cal Bernstein's cell phone, and guess what—he made multiple calls to a burner phone."

"A burner?" Terry said. "Dude, you've just upgraded Lomax's hit man theory from dumb-as-shit to not-as-stupid-as-he-made-it-sound."

"Don't jump the gun," Muller said. "A lot of regular law-abiding citizens carry burner phones."

"And a lot of smart computer cops know how to trace burner phones," Terry said. "Did you come up with anything?"

"The only thing I came up with is that whoever owned this phone knew how to cover his tracks."

"Which means Bernstein was calling an untraceable burner phone, which is definitely not what a lot of regular law-abiding citizens carry."

"That's why I said your instincts are bordering on brilliant. The problem is I don't know how to find out who owns the burner."

"Try calling it and leave a message," Terry said. "Something crafty, like, 'Hi, this is LAPD. Could you please stop by our office and help us wrap up a homicide investigation?'"

"Who did Bernstein call the day of the murder?" I asked.

"He made six calls. Three traceable and three to the burner."

"He was probably checking in with the guy who hired him," Terry said. "Who are the other three?"

"One to his daughter in Charlotte, North Carolina, and another one to his son in New York City. Both of them were under ten seconds, like maybe he just left a quick voicemail. But the last call he made went on for sixteen minutes."

"The security cameras in the parking lot caught Bernstein sitting in his car for eighteen minutes," I said. "Who did he call?

His wife?"

Muller looked down at his phone log. "No. It was a local number. Belongs to a guy in Brentwood. Bruce Bower."

Terry and I looked at each other. He picked up the folder that Apovian had just sent us. The entire Wade Yancy file wasn't much thicker than the envelope it came in.

"*Bruce Bower*?" he asked, reading the name off the top page. "Bernstein's last call was to Bruce Bower? B-O-W-E-R?"

Muller nodded.

"Congratulations, Boy Wonder," Terry said. "I think you may have just stumbled onto the answer to a rabbi's prayers."

Muller shrugged. "I don't know what I did, but apparently I did it well. Is there anything else I can do for you guys?"

"For starters," Terry said, "find out if Mr. Bower plays golf."

CHAPTER 17

MULLER SPENDS HOURS on end searching for, sifting through, and trying to make sense of mountains of data. I once told him his job was like looking for a needle in a haystack.

He laughed. "Anyone can find a needle in a haystack," he said. "All you need is a metal detector. My job is more like if someone gave you a picture of a snowflake that was taken by a black-and-white security camera in a 7-Eleven. Then they send you out in a blizzard and tell you to find that flake."

We filled him in on the Yancy case we had just inherited.

Muller is a big kid at heart, and before we were even finished, he was grinning like an eight-year-old whose mommy and daddy told him they were taking him to Disney World.

We didn't have to tell him what we wanted. We just turned him loose. He was back thirty minutes later, still smiling. "Most cop fun I've had in a long time," he said. "I started by pulling Bower's phone records. Besides calling each other, he and Bernstein have one number in common."

"Tell us it's the burner phone," Terry said.

"It's the burner phone," Muller said, a triumphant geek grin on his face. "I still can't trace it, but if Bower is dialing the same dude who you think hired Bernstein to kill the doc, then Yancy's unfortunate encounter with the Prius is looking less and less like an accident."

Terry gave him a thumbs-up. "Now tell us that Bruce Bower is a golfer."

"Bruce Bower is a golfer," Muller said, "and he's got the credit card charges for greens fees and lessons to prove it. He doesn't belong to a private club, which means he doesn't store his clubs in a locker. He has to carry them wherever he plays. Most guys just leave them in their car. It makes their lives a lot easier."

"It also comes in handy if you run someone down, and they're not quite dead," Terry said. "You just pull the old nine-iron out of the trunk, line up your shot, and swing—hole in one."

"Good job," I said.

Muller held up a hand. "Dude, I'm not nearly done. I figured if the two perps are connected, let's see if the two victims have anything in common."

"We already know that Kraus is a doc, and Yancy worked for a drug company," I said. "Did they know each other?"

"Yancy was the Vice President of Brand Development for Chilton-Winslow Pharmaceuticals. His key product areas were cardiovascular, joint care, and—you're going to love this—reproductive endocrinology, which is corporate speak for 'the guy was in charge of selling shit to fertility docs.'"

"So Kraus was Yancy's customer," I said.

"He was Yancy's *best* customer," Muller said. "But it's much more interesting than that. Did you know that Big Pharma pays doctors for using their products?"

"Isn't that illegal?"

"You mean is the government concerned that bribing a doc to use your drug instead of your competitor's could possibly cloud his medical judgment? It's illegal as hell, but if everybody out there stopped doing illegal shit, we'd all be out of work. Also, since every law has loopholes, every drug company has a team of lawyers looking for the holes. One of the ways they get around the bribery thing is by openly paying the docs consulting fees and royalties."

"Kraus is loaded," I said. "His house alone is probably worth close to twenty mil. Can you dig into his finances and find out if any came from Chilton-Winslow?"

"I've already dug. There's a government website that keeps track of how much money Big Pharma pays out to doctors. Even if the rep takes the doc out for a burger and a beer, the dollar amount has to be reported."

"And how many burgers and beers did Chilton buy for Kraus?" Terry asked.

"Last year, they paid him a little over six million dollars. Most of that was in cash, but some of it was in seminar expenses."

"Define *seminar*," I said.

"I found these on Google images," he said, tapping the screen on his iPad. "Here's one of Yancy and Kraus at a sales meeting in Rio. And here's another one—this time with their wives—on a cruise ship in the Mediterranean."

"That would be your basic floating seminar," Terry said. "You got anything else?"

"Just one more thing," Muller said, dropping his voice to a whisper. "But I had to go off the reservation to get it. It's definitely not LAPD approved, but I guarantee you it'll make you happy."

"Lay it on me," Terry said.

Muller flipped his hand up in the air and tossed something in our direction. Terry caught it and let out a whoop.

Skittles.

CHAPTER 18

TEN MINUTES AFTER Muller gave our investigation something we could actually investigate, we were summoned to Kilcullen's office.

The only vegetables in sight were in a Styrofoam cup on his desk, but the celery looked limp and the carrot sticks were dry and slightly gray from lack of attention.

"Catch me up on where you are," he said.

"We've got good news and bad news," Terry said. "No arrests yet, but we've added the possible homicide of a drug company executive to our Crimes To Solve list."

"The mayor is going to tear us a new one," Kilcullen scowled, the ugliness of his political obligations fouling his normally engaging Irish-cop smile. "Give me the good news."

"That was the good news," I said. "We just picked up a traffic accident fatality from West LA. Eli did the autopsy, and he thinks it may not be as accidental as it looks."

"Who gives a shit?" Kilcullen snapped.

"The victim worked for a drug company that paid Dr. Kraus six million dollars last year," Terry said, "so Lomax and I decided a shit was definitely worth giving."

Six million dollars was all it took for the familiar Kilcullen twinkle to return to his eyes.

"I'm listening," he said, plucking a shriveled carrot from the cup. He took a bite, tossed the rest in the wastebasket, then sat back and listened without uttering a word until we got him up to speed.

"The fact that Yancy's company was paying Kraus to pimp their drugs only confirms that the two victims were in cahoots," he said when we were done. "But lots of docs take payoffs from drug companies. Where's the motive for killing them? And if there is one, who's behind it?"

"We don't have a clue, boss, but there's a good chance Bruce Bower knows," I said. "We're going to pay him a visit and ask him some questions."

"Bad idea," he said. "If a couple of new cops show up and grill him about a traffic accident he thinks was wrapped up weeks ago, he'll know he's under suspicion."

"We're not going to say a word about Yancy," I said. "As far as Bower knows, that's not even on our radar. Our cover story is that we're doing some follow-up work on the Kraus murder, and we're contacting everyone Cal Bernstein called over the past few months. We have no idea if we'll get anything from him, but since we don't have enough evidence for a search warrant, we figure it's worth a shot."

Kilcullen responded with half a frown and zero recognition of the fact that we were one step ahead of him. "I don't know if questioning him is the best way to go," he said. "Why don't I call Mel Berger at the mayor's office and have him find us a judge who will issue a warrant as a favor?"

"Fuck Mel Berger," Terry said. "The last time you called him for a favor he never let us forget it. Do you want to call him again and tell him you can't get the job done without his muscle?"

"Terry's right," I said. "If Bower thinks he's one of dozens of people we're crossing off our list, he's not going to suspect anything, and he's not going to panic."

"Don't worry about it, boss," Terry said. "I promise I'll use every ounce of finesse I have in my body."

"They pay me to worry, Biggs. And for the record, you've got all the finesse of a rutting bull moose. Let Lomax do the talking, because all you have to do is spook this guy once, and you'll never find the smoking gun."

"Point well taken," Terry said. "And for the record, we're looking for a smoking nine-iron."

CHAPTER 19

THE BOWERS LIVED in Brentwood, which would normally put them a notch or two above the Bernsteins on the socio-economic food chain. But that was offset by the fact that their house was just off Sepulveda, where the noise and the fumes of the 405 freeway made it one of the least desirable areas of their affluent zip code.

"According to the accident report, they were driving from here to Century City to get ice cream," Terry said as soon as he parked in front of their one-story bungalow on Homedale Street. "I can understand making a forty-minute round trip to score weed, but who the hell drives that far for raspberry ripple?"

"Great question," I said. "That should be at the top of the list of things you don't ask them."

"I know the rules, Mike. I'm just pointing out the obvious."

"And to quote a sage Irish philosopher, you point with all the finesse of a rutting pig."

"Rutting bull moose," Terry corrected.

"Aha! You *were* paying attention," I said. "I believe our supreme leader also advised you to 'let Lomax do the talking,' so if your mouth suddenly goes on autopilot, pop a few Skittles in there to keep it busy."

"You really expect me to do my job without talking?" he said as we walked up the driveway.

"Why not? Harpo Marx made a dozen movies—never said a word."

"Harpo had a horn he could honk," he grumbled.

I rang the doorbell, and an attractive, fiftyish woman greeted us with a smile which disappeared as soon as I flashed my shield and said, "LAPD. Is Bruce Bower at home?"

People with nothing to hide are often intrigued, even delighted, to have a cop drag them away from their humdrum routine. I've had more than one person joke about who they'd like to play them in the movie version of our brief interview.

But this woman did not appear to be intrigued, and she certainly wasn't delighted. "Bruce is not well. I'm his wife Claire. Can I help?" she said, her body tense, her defense mechanisms on point.

"We're doing some follow-up on a shooting that happened yesterday, ma'am," I said. "We're going through the shooter's cell phone records, and we're sorry to disturb you, but we have to touch base with everyone he spoke to recently."

"You mean Cal Bernstein?" she said, looking somewhat relieved. "Terrible, terrible thing. We saw it on TV. Bruce was very upset."

"It won't take long, ma'am. Just a few routine questions," I said, doing my best to sound like a TV cop who has to do a quick scene with a minor character before he gets to confront the real killer. "But if Mr. Bower isn't feeling well, we can come back another time. We've got a lot of people to check off our list."

I only gave her two options. Answer *a few routine questions* and get it over with in a hurry. Or send us away and have the specter of a police investigation hanging over her head. I had no doubt which one she'd take.

"Come in," she said, leading us into the living room.

The man sitting on the sofa didn't look much like the picture on Bruce Bower's driver's license. He'd aged about twenty years, his skin was dry and papery, and his hair was gone. Not just the curly mop of silver gray on his head, but his eyebrows, lashes, and most likely, his pubic hair as well.

I knew the look. I'd lived with it while Joanie was dying. The ravages of chemo.

"Bruce, the police are here to ask you some questions about Cal Bernstein," she said.

He nodded. "Terrible, terrible thing. We saw it on TV," he said, echoing his wife word for word.

"Were you two close?" I asked.

"Close?" he said, his voice as frail as the frame it was coming from. "I've only known him a few months, but you could say we had become kind of chummy."

"Where'd you meet him?"

A simple question, but he rubbed his hand across his chin, vetting the answer in his head before he spoke. "A support group. Cal and I were both dying of cancer. I guess he beat me to it."

"I'm sorry to hear about your illness," I said. "What else can you tell us about this support group?"

"It's called Living With Dying," he said, looking at his wife. "Every Monday, Wednesday, and Friday night at eight a bunch of people who are gearing up for the final curtain meet in the basement of Our Lady of Mercy Church in Santa Monica and talk." He looked back at us. "You probably think it's depressing as hell, but we all have a lot of laughs."

"It's true," Claire said. "Bruce always comes back from those meetings so energized."

"Did Mr. Bernstein ever talk about killing anyone?"

"Did he ever talk about killing anyone?" Bower repeated. "Of course not."

Cops have built-in lie detectors, and between their body language and their verbal choices, the Bowers had given up about half a dozen tells that they were either dancing around the truth or flat-out lying.

"Do you have any idea why he'd shoot Dr. Kraus?" I asked.

"The man had a brain tumor," Claire said, grabbing the question as her husband fumbled for an answer.

"Good point, good point," Bruce said. "I'm not a doctor, but I would guess that could screw up somebody's thinking and make him do crazy things."

I nodded like they'd made perfect sense. "Thank you both for your help. We're sorry for your troubles and wish you both the best."

Claire escorted us to the front step. "That was very taxing for my husband," she said. "I hope you won't be needing him anymore."

"No, ma'am," I said. "We've got everything we need for our report."

"So, Detective Biggs," I said as soon as we were on the road, "Cal Bernstein is terminal and kills Dr. Kraus. Now it turns out that the man who accidentally mowed down Wade Yancy also has one foot in the grave. I don't believe in coincidence, and I know a dozen judges who don't believe in it either. What's your take?"

Terry ran an imaginary zipper across his lips and made the turn from Homedale to Thurston.

"All right, I get it," I said. "You behaved very well. You can talk now."

He turned to me, lolled out his tongue, puffed up his cheeks, crossed his eyes, and mimed a perfect, signature Harpo Marx Gookie face.

"You fucking clown," I said, laughing. "Just for that, I'm going to the Living With Dying meeting tonight without you."

He took both hands off the wheel, folded them in front of his chest, and begged mock forgiveness.

"Fine," I said. "I have a five o'clock doctor's appointment. Pick me up at my house about a quarter to eight."

He pumped his fist, grinned like an idiot, and honked the horn incessantly as we drove up Sunset.

Terry Biggs cracks me up. Even when he doesn't say a word.

CHAPTER 20

"DROP ME OFF right here," I said as Terry pulled into the Hollywood station parking lot. "I'm not going into the office. I have just enough time to make it to this doctor's appointment."

"You want me to go with you?" he asked as we got out of his car.

"No."

"Are you sure? It'll be a lot more laughs if you take me with you."

"Thanks, but no thanks," I said, getting into my car. "I'll see you later."

"Good luck," he said as I pulled out of the lot and onto Wilcox.

I turned on the CD player, but I was no longer in the mood to be transported to a happier place by filling the car with music from a happier time. I killed the sound so I could make my way into the most dangerous neighborhood I know. Inside my head.

My thoughts immediately turned to mortality. Mine, Joanie's, Bruce Bower's, and of course, Cal Bernstein's. Cal had lived, laughed, loved, worked, played, and made his mark on this planet for fifty-four years. And I had been completely unaware of him until the last few seconds of his existence.

But his death hit me hard.

And now it was gnawing its way into my consciousness, reminding me of the words of wisdom I'd heard last night from an eight-year-old. *We all die, Mike. The best thing to do is have as much fun with your life while you can.*

Maybe Sophie was right. Maybe knowing that death is in the wings drives most of us to make the most out of the time we have on stage.

But still, I thought. *Dying sucks, and I'm not ready.*

An hour later, I was in yet another exam room, wearing yet another totally useless hospital gown, with my ass the target of yet another doctor.

This time there was no gunfire to interrupt the procedure, and Dr. Abordo jammed an industrial-sized needle into my hip bone. Despite the fact that he'd given me a local anesthetic, it hurt like hell.

"Sorry," he said. "Take some Tylenol if you're in pain when the anesthetic wears off."

"I can live with the pain. What I can't live with is the suspense."

"The lab usually takes five days," he said as he bandaged the site. "Doug Heller will call you with the results."

"Doug will only give me the cold hard facts. I was hoping you could find it in your heart to tell me the possibilities. Five days is a long time to be in the dark."

Herand Abordo was young, affable, and after the initial doctor/new patient foreplay, I got the feeling that he'd be more forthcoming than most. But I knew I'd have to press him for it.

"What would you like to know?" he said.

"For starters, what the hell is splenomegaly? I saw you write it in my chart."

"I'm amazed you can read my handwriting right side up, much less upside down, but all it means is that your spleen is enlarged. I thought Doug told you that."

"He did. Of course, I have no idea what a spleen is or what it does, but it's gratifying to know that I'll have the biggest one in the boy's locker room."

He laughed. I'd have to tell Terry that he wasn't the only funny cop in the squad.

"Seriously, Doc. Is it leukemia? Should I—what's the phrase you guys use—get my affairs in order?"

"Jesus, Mike—slow down. First of all, only the lab can tell us if it's leukemia. If it is, you have treatment options. As for getting your affairs in order, absolutely not. Just do what you always do. Enjoy your life. Start tonight. Do you have anything fun planned?"

"Yeah," I said. "It should be a lot of fun."

"Excellent," he said.

I didn't have the heart to tell him that my big plans for the evening were to go to my first Living With Dying meeting.

CHAPTER 21

DRIVING HOME I stressed out over who I should tell about my elevated blood count, my enlarged spleen, and my uncertain future.

It was Wednesday night. Tomorrow was Sophie's welcome-home party for Carly. And since I wouldn't get the verdict back from the lab for five days, there was no sense sabotaging anybody else's weekend.

I felt rotten about holding out on Diana, but her husband had died a few years ago, and I knew that if I told her about the bone marrow biopsy she would jump to the illogical conclusion that I was next.

On the other hand, keeping it a secret from my father was not only an easy call, it was a blessed relief. If Big Jim even had an inkling that I could possibly have cancer, he would bombard me with a litany of specialists I should see, homeopathic remedies I should try, and stories of medical miracles meant to inspire me to a state of physical and spiritual well-being.

I love my father, but his unsolicited advice and well-intentioned meddling would turn five days of waiting for the lab results into an eternity.

Decision made: *I would suffer in silence.*

But as soon as I turned onto Hill Street, I realized that silence wasn't in the cards. There was a white stretch limo parked in front of my house. Behind that was a big ugly food truck that my brother Frankie and his girlfriend Izzy had cleverly dubbed The Big Ugly Food Truck.

I parked, opened the front door to the house, and braced myself for the onslaught of my loving family.

"Where the hell have you been?" Big Jim bellowed. "We were about to start the party without you."

Sophie was right beside him. "No we weren't," she said. "Large James has no patience. I made him wait."

"Thanks for waiting, but I thought the party for your mom was tomorrow night."

"It is," Big Jim said. "This is the party for people who are planning tomorrow's party. Have a seat."

"It's been a long day, Dad, and it's not over. Do you really need my help?"

"Hell, no. We don't need your help. Sophie and I just want to regale you with what we've cooked up and watch you fall down in awe of our party-planning prowess."

"Regale in a hurry," I said. "What's the limo doing out front?"

"That's the official vehicle for the homecoming queen," Sophie said. "I decorated the inside. You can't see it till tomorrow."

"I'll count the minutes. And what's Frankie's big ugly food truck doing here?"

"Because Frankie and me, we are *los cocineros*," a female voice answered.

I turned around. It was Isabella, my brother's girlfriend, business partner, and according to Big Jim, the person most responsible for helping Frankie keep both feet on the ground. Sophie loved her. I loved her. Hell, everybody loved her. Frankie most of all.

"Izzy," I said, kissing her on each cheek. "Congratulations. I wondered who Sophie was going to hire to take on the culinary gig for this momentous homecoming fiesta."

"Are you kidding?" Izzy said. "Me and Frankie, we beat out a dozen other big ugly food trucks."

Sophie had a mouth-wide-open grin. "It was a tough choice," she said, her eyes dancing around the room, from me to Big Jim to Izzy and back, "but I decided to keep it in the family."

"Cómo estás, mi hermano?" It was Frankie, holding out two beers. He passed me one and gave me a big bro hug.

"I don't know how you say 'beat to hell' in Español, but that's how I am, and to make it worse, Terry and I have to go out tonight to follow up on a lead."

"Oh, Mike, not tonight." It was Diana. She and Big Jim's wife Angel came out of the kitchen, each with a glass of white wine in hand.

"Yes tonight," I said, giving her a kiss. "I cleared the decks for tomorrow night, but nobody warned me about the party before the party."

"How well do you know your father?" Angel said, moving in for my final welcome-home kiss. "Even worse, he's corrupted this poor little girl. She's picking up all his bad habits. Carly will see what he's done, and she'll probably never let us near Sophie again."

"More likely she'll thank us," Big Jim boomed. "It takes a village, and we all did a bang-up job of helping raise this little troublemaker while Carly was in China. Especially you, Mike." He capped the compliment with the ultimate Big Jim gesture of gratitude. A genuine, old-fashioned *attaboy*. He slapped me on the back.

The shock reverberated through my body, seared my brain, and took my breath away. Six inches lower and he'd have connected with the exact spot where the horse syringe had drilled a hole in my bone, and I'd have passed out cold.

My eyes watered, and I sucked hard on the beer bottle to help drown out the pain. It didn't help.

"I have to take a bio break," I said. "I'll be right back."

I practically staggered to the bathroom, but the fun quotient in the room was too high for any of them to notice.

Still dressed, I sat down on the toilet seat to let the pain subside. It didn't. There was no Tylenol in the medicine cabinet, but there was a bottle of Advil. I popped two and washed them down with beer. I lowered my pants and looked at the bandage on my hip. No blood. Just a million nerve endings screaming in agony. I took a third Advil, thought about a fourth, then decided to give the first three time to kick in.

I put on my happy face and rejoined the party planners. "I'll bet there's one thing you didn't get for this shindig," I said.

"What?" Sophie challenged.

"The Rockettes."

"Ha!" she said. "We *did* get them. Only we got the LA Rockettes."

"I thought the Rockettes only worked in New York, and they're called the Rockettes because Radio City Music Hall is in Rockefeller Center."

"Well, our Rockettes work for Big Jim's Trucking Company."

I looked at my father.

He nodded. "She's right. You know them as Chico, Freddie, Rufus, and Otto. But tomorrow night, when they put on their dancing shoes and kick up their heels, they're going to be The Truckettes. It's going to be a night this little girl will never forget for the rest of her life."

He was right. But in all the wrong ways.

CHAPTER 22

"DO YOU KNOW how many different support groups there are in LA?" Terry asked as we drove to the Living With Dying meeting.

"I have no idea," I said.

"Take a wild guess. Just toss out a number."

"Eighty-three."

"More like a thousand and eighty-three. Mike, I went online. If you have an addiction, an affliction, a disease, a disorder, a habit, a handicap—whatever the hell is mucking up your life, there's a bunch of other people mucking up their lives the exact same way. So what do they do? They get together in a church basement somewhere and talk each other out of the muck."

"I know. Kilcullen's been sober for twenty-five years. And if it weren't for Gamblers Anonymous, my brother Frankie would be living under a bridge somewhere, if he were alive at all. Maybe the reason there are so many of those support groups is because they work."

"That's what I'm getting at. You have a problem, you get together with likeminded people, and you fix it. It's such a good idea that I've started my own support group—Cops Without Yachts. You want in?"

Terry doesn't just dream about going into stand-up comedy after he leaves LAPD, he works at it. Half a dozen support-group jokes later, we pulled into the parking lot at Our Lady of Mercy.

It was 7:56. We waited in the car and watched people shuffle down the stairs or take the handicap ramp to the basement. At eight on the nose, we walked in just as the meeting was getting under way.

The space was brightly lit and cheerful, with one entire wall covered with artwork drawn by kids who used the facility during school hours. Terry and I took seats in the rear, and I did a head count. Twenty-two people—three in wheelchairs, and three more wearing nasal cannulas hooked up to portable oxygen tanks. Almost everyone was either bald, balding, or wearing a hat.

The leader, sitting at the teacher's desk in the front of the room, spoke. "Hey, everybody, my name is Charlie Brock, I'm forty-four years old, and I'm living with hepatocellular carcinoma, or as I like to say after three drinks—liver cancer."

Everyone responded with a chorus of "Hi, Charlie."

"I see a few new faces, so for those of you who are joining us for the first time, this is the Colorado Avenue chapter of Living With Dying. We don't have a lot of rules, and except for the flight of stairs you walked down to get here, we don't have any steps to follow. We've all been diagnosed with a terminal illness, and while some of us are destined to stick around longer than others, we all know that we're leaving the party before it's over.

"That, my friends, can be a real bummer, so we meet here three nights a week to get un-bummed. We're all dying, but our primary mission is to help each other focus on living. Which means nobody wants to hear you bitch and moan if your Social Security check was late, or if you saw a roach in your kitchen—unless said roach is the ass end of a joint—which, God bless Prop 215, has been legal for folks like us since 1996."

Several heads in front of me nodded enthusiastically. California's Compassionate Use Act allowing the use of medical cannabis was a significant victory for every chemo patient in the room.

"So that's how these meetings work," Charlie continued. "We

know that you're dying, but what we want to hear about is how you're living. Did you paint a picture, build a birdhouse, drink an amusing little pinot grigio, get laid, write a song? Who wants to share first?"

Hands shot up, and Charlie pointed at an African-American man.

"My name is Rupert Simms," he said. "I'm sixty-seven years old, I'm living with lung cancer, and I wrote a song about getting laid."

The group laughed and called out, "Hi, Rupert." Terry joined in, one class clown supporting another.

"I just got back from Baltimore, Atlanta, Kansas City, and Houston," Rupert said, his voice rough and gravelly from his disease. "I've got a brother, two sisters, four kids, eleven grandkids, and a boatload of nieces and nephews. I love most of them, I ain't too keen on a few of them, but I wanted to say goodbye to all of them. I figured if the Grateful Dead could do a farewell tour of America, why not the Grateful-I-Ain't-Dead-Yet?"

Rupert then proceeded to captivate the room with highlights of his journey, the details of which were both shamelessly funny and painfully poignant. I got so caught up in his story that I stopped thinking about why I was there and let my mind drift to thoughts of Joanie, who like Rupert, lived her dying days to the fullest. She'd have enjoyed hanging out with him.

"Best two weeks of my life," he said, wrapping it up. "I want to thank all of you for teaching me how to focus on living instead of dying, and I want to thank my higher power for giving me the strength and the bus fare to do it."

Everyone applauded, including me and Terry. Hands went up again, and Charlie pointed to a woman, but I never heard her name. I was too busy eyeballing the latecomer who had just come in. It was Bruce Bower.

He walked quietly toward the back row, saw me and Terry, and panicked. But he was too far in to bolt and too close to pretend not to see us. He nodded a perfunctory hello, then sat off to the side and several rows in front of us.

The meeting hummed along. Almost everyone shared. But not Bruce.

When the hour was almost up, Terry leaned toward me and whispered. "I guess old Brucie boy figured it out on his own. We didn't even have to tell him."

"Tell him what?" I whispered back.

"He has the right to remain silent."

CHAPTER 23

THE CLOCK ON the wall read 8:59 when Charlie took the floor again. "We lost one of our own this week," he said. "Cal Bernstein. We'll be giving Cal the usual sendoff at Halligan's tonight, and in keeping with LWD tradition, all of our serious drinking will be accompanied by sharing memories of his life, not focusing on his passing. Let's close the meeting with a moment of silent prayer for Cal."

Heads bowed, the room went still, and my mind replayed the scene of a desperate man with the barrel of a shotgun under his chin. He had urged me to walk away. Warned me not to look. But I couldn't, and now the final frame of Cal Bernstein's existence is forever burned into my memory bank.

"Amen," Charlie finally said, snapping me back into the moment. "I hope to see all of you back here again on Friday."

The meeting broke up, and Bruce Bower was the first one out of his chair. He wasted no time getting to the front of the room. He whispered something to Charlie, who nodded, looked up at me and Terry, waved, then headed our way. Bruce followed reluctantly.

"Detectives," Charlie said, extending a hand. "I'm Charlie Brock. Bruce just informed me that you're with LAPD, but I told him I knew that the minute you walked through the door."

"Is it that obvious we're cops?" I said, shaking his hand.

Charlie laughed. "Heck no. I saw you on TV," he said, pointing at me. "Bruce just told me you swung by his place this afternoon to talk about Cal. If you have any questions for the rest of us, come on over to the bar and ask away. The problem is, I can't imagine that any of us will have any answers that will help. You sat through this meeting. What Cal did is the exact opposite of what we believe in."

"How well did you know him?" I asked.

"I didn't know him long, Detective," Charlie said, "but when two people are thrown together the way Cal and I were, you learn a lot about each other in a very short time. The two of us would go out for a couple of pops after the meeting. Plus, we talked on the phone a couple of times a week."

"What did you talk about?"

"Anything and everything. Mostly guy stuff—sports, TV shows, politics, women. Sometimes, especially on the weekends when there were no meetings, we would talk upbeat stuff about our lives, past and present, just to help each other stay positive. The thing is, people in this program talk a blue streak. It's like being in a lifeboat. Sometimes you've got nothing better to do than to jaw with the other guy in the boat. And sometimes it's because you've got something you don't want to take to the grave, and you need someone to pour your heart out to."

"Like confession?" Terry, the lapsed Catholic, asked.

"Cal was Jewish," Charlie said, grinning. "I don't think he was too big into confession. I'm talking more about getting shit off your chest."

"Did Cal say anything to you about having a grudge against Dr. Kraus?"

"Not to me. How about you?" he asked Bruce.

Bruce shook his head.

"One of the things you learn when you get here is not to dredge up resentments from the past," Charlie said. "The cancer is eating away at my liver fast enough. If I dig up some old grudge, it's going to start festering and destroy my liver that much faster. LWD teaches us not to ruminate about yesterday or worry about tomorrow. You know what they say—you've got to take it one day at a time."

"You mean like Alcoholics Anonymous," Terry said.

"Kind of, but there are two differences," Charlie said. "AA helps people recover from alcoholism so they can get on with their lives. But recovery isn't in the cards for us."

"What's the second difference?" I said.

"The people in Alcoholics Anonymous don't get to go out for drinks after their meetings. We do." He winked. "Every storm has a rainbow. Come on, I'll buy you guys the first round."

CHAPTER 24

HALLIGAN'S WAS EVERY bit the Irish pub I thought it would be. Wooden floors, brick accents, cozy lighting, and a burly bartender who gave a shout-out to Charlie and his entourage as we came through the door.

In addition to Charlie and Bruce, there were seven others in the LWD contingent, all anxious to either toast their dead comrade or drink their fears into oblivion.

As soon as Charlie explained who we were and why we were there, the guiding principal of Living With Dying went out the window. Everybody wanted to focus on Cal's death, especially once they knew that I had witnessed his demise.

It's human nature. The more grisly the crime, the more details people want. It's what sells supermarket tabloids.

We sat them all down at a large table, then asked Rupert to join us at a booth in the back.

Charlie was blindsided. "I thought we were doing this all together," he said. "You know—a group grope."

"I wish we could," Terry said, "but there's a difference between a support group meeting and a police investigation. You know what *we* say? One witness at a time."

Rupert, who had been open and forthcoming at the meeting, was guarded sitting across from us. I got the feeling he was a people person, but not if those people were cops. "You think I know anything about Cal Bernstein shooting that doctor?" he asked.

"No," Terry said. "If you do, it would help, but we're more interested in what you can tell us about the shooter."

He nodded. "What do you want to know?"

"What was he like?"

"Bernstein? He was kind of a broken record. Whenever he shared, he would try to start out with something positive, like 'I saw a good movie,' or some shit like that, but mostly he was a Negative Nancy, always kicking himself for missing the boat."

"What boat?"

"He thought he was going to be a hotshot lawyer, but he flunked out of school and wound up bouncing from one dead-end job to another. The only time I had a drink with him I told him I ain't going to die rich either, but at least I can die with a smile on my face. He looks at me and says, 'You don't get it.' Fuck him. Life is too short to waste on whiners. Are we done here?"

We were done. The other interviews went just as fast. None of the other six people were close with Cal, and nobody had anything to hide. Nobody except Charlie and Bruce.

We thanked them all and left.

"Charlie Brock is a much better liar than Bruce," Terry said as he made a U-turn on Colorado Avenue. "His big mistake was when he stopped lying to us. That warm and fuzzy tale about him and Cal talking on the phone is one hundred percent true, and it's going to bury him before the cancer does."

"As soon as he got going about how the two of them were phone buddies, it was all I could do to not give you a high five," I said. "I'll bet they talked a lot. There's only one problem. The phone company doesn't have any record of Cal's phone connecting to any number that belongs to Charlie."

"Charlie is our man with the burner phone," Terry said. "And if you had any doubt, did you see Bruce race up to the front to tell him that Five-0 was in the house?"

"We still don't have a motive," I said. "We've got some interesting puzzle pieces—two dead guys connected to Chilton-Winslow and two terminal killers, but we have no clue why this is all going down."

"Or who's behind it," Terry said. "Charlie Brock is a soldier, a handler to work Bruce and Cal, but nothing about him says he's running the show. First thing tomorrow morning, let's have Muller run a background check on him."

"How about second thing tomorrow morning," I said. "If we're lucky, first thing will be somebody slapping a search warrant in our hands."

Terry turned onto Pico Boulevard, and I folded my arms across my chest, tilted my head back, and closed my eyes. I'd had enough talking for one day.

"I relate to that whole living with dying concept," Terry said, ignoring my cue.

"How so?"

"Think about it, Mike. Death and dying is what we do every day. We're never going to be immune to it, but we're comfortable talking about it."

"You are so fucking transparent," I said, opening my eyes. "There's nothing to talk about. I said what I had to say when I came back from meeting with Eli."

"That was eight hours ago. Since then you went to see the hematologist. What did he say?"

"He said it's going to be five days before we know anything, and in the meantime I should make the most of every day and just have fun."

"In that case, you have had a fabulous day. You started out this morning at the morgue, and you ended with a room full of people who are getting ready to take the big dirt nap," he said. "If you work homicide, it doesn't get any more fun than that."

CHAPTER 25

"IS THAT ALL you're going to order?" Charlie asked.

"I can barely drink this," Bruce said. "I'm too nervous."

"About what?" Charlie said, digging into a bowl of caramel apple crisp.

The two of them had left Halligan's and driven to a Denny's on Lincoln Boulevard.

"*About what*? About those two cops. First they came to my house, then to the meeting. They know something."

"Bruce, they know that Cal shot the fertility doc. That's what they're investigating."

Bruce took a deep breath. The herbal tea he'd ordered was lukewarm at best. "So you don't think I fucked up?" he asked, taking a sip.

"You? No. But Cal? He fucked up big time. The instructions were simple. Make it look like an accident. In what universe is walking into a doctor's office and gunning him down supposed to look like anything but Murder One? Did you know that he called me the night before he killed the doc?"

"No. About what?"

"He was making me promise for the hundredth time that his wife would get paid after he did the deed. I kept telling him not to worry, this is a well-funded operation. As soon as the news breaks that Kraus is dead, the money will be wired to her account. That calmed him down. He said it would happen soon. But did he tell me he was going to burst into a crowded medical office with his gun blazing? If he had, I'd have pulled the plug on the whole deal. But he didn't say a word, and now we're caught up in a goddamn murder investigation."

"So does that mean his wife isn't getting paid?" Bruce asked, taking another taste of the tepid tea.

"If it were up to me, I wouldn't give her a dime," Charlie said. "Plus, I'd make her give back the advance money. But it's not my call. The boss isn't happy about how it all went down, but a deal's a deal, and the money is being wired to Cal's widow as we speak."

"Claire's already got her money. It takes a big load off my mind."

Charlie wiped a trail of vanilla ice cream and caramel goo from his chin. "Then I guess you can rest in peace."

"What do you think the cops asked Rupert and the others?"

"The same shit they asked us. Do you have any idea why Cal shot the doc?"

"Do you think they asked them anything about..." Bruce looked around the diner and lowered his voice. "About me running down Yancy?"

"Bruce—did they ask you about it?"

"No."

"Then it's not on their radar. And you know why it's not on their radar? Because you got it right. Homicide cops don't investigate traffic accidents."

"That's what Claire said. She said they're only here about Kraus. They don't even know about Yancy."

Charlie focused on spooning up the dregs of the cream and the remaining bits of brown sugar crumble.

"How can you eat that poison?" Bruce said. "Did you see the nutritional facts on the menu? Seven hundred and forty calories. Eighty-nine grams of—"

Charlie let go of his spoon. "What the fuck did you just say Claire said about Yancy?"

"Nothing. I didn't say anything."

"Bullshit, Bruce. You said Claire said the cops don't even know about Yancy."

"And they don't."

"But why would your wife even think that a traffic accident you had three weeks ago would be of any interest to two homicide detectives?"

"I don't know, Charlie. Feminine logic. Who knows how they think?"

Charlie leaned across the table. "Claire knows it wasn't an accident, doesn't she?"

"That's ridiculous."

"You're lying to me. When did you tell her? Better yet, *why* did you tell her?"

Bruce tried to pick up his tea cup, but his hands were jumping like spit on a griddle. Tears welled up in his eyes. "I had to tell her. I couldn't do it alone."

Charlie's eyes widened. "She *went* with you?"

"She kept me calm. I mean, I'm new at this murder shit. Plus, she was great with the cop when he interviewed us after."

"So *you* didn't go by the rules either."

"Whoa. Wait a minute, Charlie. Don't make it sound like I screwed up like Cal did. *I* went by the rules. I *made* it look like an accident."

"But you weren't supposed to tell Claire."

"Don't you think that's a pretty asinine rule? There's half a million in a bank in the Caymans in her name. She'd have figured it out whether I told her or not. As far as I'm concerned, I earned my money. And if you give me another few weeks, I'll be dead, and I'll have held up my end of the bargain."

Charlie nodded slowly and smiled. "In that case, neither of us have anything to worry about."

CHAPTER 26

I WAS UP before dawn and out the door in twenty minutes. As much as I hated to skip my morning ritual with Sophie on her last day as our live-in daughter, I had no choice. Search warrants, especially one as hard to come by as this one, are best executed while the judge's signature is still wet.

At 6:30, Terry and I were back on Homedale Street ringing the Bower's doorbell. Claire, wearing a robe, opened the door. She was surprised as hell to see us and even more surprised to see eight more cops behind us.

I handed her the warrant and the search team spread out.

The usual scenario followed. Outrage, protest, threats. We'd seen it all before. The suspect-as-victim hurling F-bombs, screaming hysterically that her civil rights were being violated, and vowing that Terry and I would be out of a job before day's end. We ignored her.

Bruce could not. He entered the room, fully dressed, smoking a cigarette. He had the good sense not to try to stop us or in any way interfere with the search. He put his arm around his wife and led her to their bedroom.

"Stay with them," Terry said to a uniform. If there was any evidence of a crime buried in the house, our job was to make sure the Bowers didn't have an opportunity to destroy it.

"Lomax! Biggs!" The call came less than five minutes after

we'd stormed through the door.

It was Jessica Keating. Any rookie can identify a bloody kitchen knife, but if you find a golf club, you need a forensic specialist to tell you whether it's a murder weapon or just another nine-iron.

Jess was waiting for us in the garage. The trunk of Bruce Bower's Prius was open, and a set of golf clubs was spread out on the concrete floor. One of her assistants sprayed luminol on the metal heads.

"Lights," she said, and the place went dark. Well, almost dark. A blue glow emanated from one of the clubs.

"It's not exactly a smoking gun," she said, "but if it's even got a smidge of Wade Yancy's DNA, I know a prosecuting attorney who's going to love slapping a tag on it that says Exhibit A."

The lights went back on, and Terry bent down to get a closer look. "I'll be damned," he said. "It *was* a nine-iron. I will never doubt Eli again."

"How long till you can tell us if it's a match?" I asked Jess.

"And before you answer," Terry said, "I just want you to know that I watched a cop show on TV last night, and they got DNA results during the commercial break."

Jessica laughed. "In real life, I can get top-line data for you in forty-eight hours. But I'll bet if I send Eli a mold of that club head, it'll take him five minutes to see if it matches the dent in Wade Yancy's skull."

"Fantastic," Terry said. He turned to me. "Come on, Lomax, let's go share the good news with Claire and Bruce."

They were waiting for us in the living room. Claire had changed from her bathrobe to her going-off-to-the-slammer outfit.

Terry had taken a vow of silence the first time we met with the Bowers, so I let him do the honors. "Claire and Bruce Bower," he said, his voice dramatic and commanding, "you are under arrest for the murder of Wade Yancy." He then read them their rights, slowly and with authority, relishing every word of it.

As soon as we cuffed them, Bruce protested. "Don't arrest her. I did it. I'll sign a confession. It was all me. Claire had nothing to do with it."

"Noble gesture, Mr. Bower," I said, "but that's not what it says on the accident report. I don't know which one of you took the chip shot that killed Yancy, but you were definitely playing as a twosome."

Bruce started sobbing, but Claire stood ramrod stiff and silent. She'd been caught, and her transformation from anger and denial to total acceptance was immediate. She remained motionless and expressionless, waiting for someone to tell her what to do.

Two uniformed officers took her by the elbows and led her to the front door. Two more escorted Bruce. Terry and I recruited two more cops to stay behind and secure the premises, then we took up the rear of the perp walk.

"I'm calling Eli," I said.

The sun was just coming up as we got outside. Eli wouldn't be at work yet, but I had his cell phone. He answered on the first ring.

"Mike," he said, "if you're calling me at this hour there can only be one reason. You found the golf club, and you called to tell me how smart I am."

"Eli," I said, heading toward the car, "you already know how smart you are, but for those who don't, there will be a front page story to that effect in tomorrow's *LA Times*. Congratu—"

The first gunshot rang out, and I instinctively dropped the phone, reached for my gun, and hit the paving-stone walkway. A second shot followed, and I heard a cop call out, "Suspect has been hit. She's down."

Terry dropped right beside me, as another cop yelled, "Mine is down too. He's bleeding bad. Calling for a bus and backup."

The shots had come from the east. I rolled onto the lawn looking for the shooter and was blinded by the morning sun.

"Is anybody in a position to see anything?" I yelled out.

I got a chorus of negative responses, heavy on the profanity.

I got into a crouch. I doubted if any of the cops were on the shooter's hit list, but I wasn't quite ready to stand up and put my theory to the test. I waddled toward where Bruce was lying on the ground. He'd been hit in the stomach. Two cops were working on him, trying to compress the wound and keep him from bleeding out.

Claire was in even worse shape. She was still alive, but she'd taken a bullet to the head. I'd seen people survive head shots, but very few, and those who do recover have a long painful road that almost always ends in a life that is forever defined by their brain injury.

Four of the cops had raced up Homedale after the shooter. One by one, they returned empty-handed.

I heard sirens approaching. Terry and I stood. "Our backup is here," I said. "At this point they're not going to do us much good. And ambulances, which probably won't do Claire Bower much good either."

"On the plus side," Terry said, "if Bruce's wound is clean, and infection doesn't set in, they could probably save his life. That ought to give him at least another three, four more weeks to keep on living with dying."

PART TWO

BAD PHARMA

CHAPTER 27

THERE'S A FRIENDLY, and sometimes not so friendly, interdepartmental rivalry between the cops and firefighters of Los Angeles. But as Terry and I watched a pair of red rescue ambulances sweep down on the crime scene, there was no denying how much LAFD means for the safety and well being of our city. As Terry so elegantly put it, "These fuckers know their shit."

Even before his unit rolled to a stop, one paramedic was out the door, sprinted to the two victims, and made a life-and-death call on the spot. "Load and go," he yelled.

There was nothing they could do for Claire or Bruce on the street. Their best chance for survival was in the OR.

The road docs lifted their charges onto backboards, and with the precision and grace of a drill team, double-timed them to separate vehicles. Doors slammed, sirens screamed, and a convoy of wailing fire trucks and cop cars sped off toward Ronald Reagan UCLA Medical Center.

"If you're going to get shot," I said as we barreled across Montana Avenue behind the red rescue wagons, "it doesn't hurt to live five minutes away from the best Level 1 Trauma Center in the city."

"I think you drank too much of the Kool-Aid at last night's Living With Dying lovefest," Terry yelled over the din of multiple sirens. "It wouldn't matter if those people had the Mayo

Clinic in their basement. They're fucked."

"Sorry for being so positive," I snapped back. "My idiot doctor told me to keep looking on the bright side of life, then call him in five days to find out if it worked."

"Mike, you'll be fine. They won't. I just hope one of them lives long enough to tell us who's the brains and the money behind this operation."

"It's not Charlie Brock," I said. "You were right last night. He's a soldier, and five bucks says he was assigned to the mop-up operation this morning. Eliminate the Bowers before the cops put the rubber hose to them."

There were at least ten doctors and nurses waiting for us in the parking lot as soon as we rolled into UCLA Med. The paramedics had done what they could on the ride over—calling in vitals, administering oxygen, containing the bleeding, and in Claire's case, putting the paddles to her chest to restart her heart.

There was one thing they couldn't do. A young paramedic jumped out of the lead truck and ran toward us. He clasped his hands together and held them in the air. "Bracelets," he yelled.

The Bowers were still in handcuffs.

"Do you mind unlocking the hardware?" he said. "I promise they won't get away."

I tossed him the key. The Bowers were uncuffed, transferred to gurneys, and just like on TV, the entire medical team raced down the corridor of the ER and wheeled them into a trauma bay.

That's as far as Terry and I could go. A surgeon in scrubs asked us for a top-line, and we gave it to her, including the ugly reality of Bruce's Stage IV lung cancer.

"Not my department," she said. "I'm just here to save his life. After that, God and the LAPD can sort it out."

"Doc," Terry said, blocking her path. "They're both murder suspects. How soon can we question them?"

"Her? A week, a month, but more likely, never. Him? Maybe tomorrow, but only if you get out of my way and let me do my job."

Terry got out of her way.

"Leave your number with security," she said, hurrying off to save a murderer. "They'll call you when he's *compos mentis*."

"Bummer," Terry said as we headed toward the lobby.

"I know," I said. "Whatever they did, they didn't deserve to be mowed down like that."

"I'm not talking about them. I'm talking about our investigation. Which one of us is going to break the news to the mayor that we had two suspects in custody, but we let them get—"

My phone rang. "Hold that complaint, Biggs." I took the call.

"Who loves you?" the female voice on the other end said.

"Officer Mulvey," I said. "What can I do for you on this beautiful October morning."

"Can you run right over? There's a woman at the station who needs the kind of warmth and comforting that you do so well."

Eileen Mulvey is happily married, but she never gets tired of flirting. "Sorry, Mulvey," I said. "I'm in an extremely depressing setting at the moment, and my warmth and comforting skills have been depleted. You'll have to satisfy your own needs."

"Not me, dumbass," Mulvey said. "There's an emotionally distraught woman here, and she insists that you and Biggs are the only ones who can help her."

"Oh. Did you get her name?"

"Multiple times," Mulvey said. "It's Janice Bernstein."

"Janice... she's Cal Bernstein's wife."

"Yes, she mentioned that several times as well."

"Do you have any idea what she wants?"

"She said she knows why her husband killed Dr. Kraus, and she'd like to share her little secret with you."

CHAPTER 28

WHEN JOANIE DIED after a long debilitating illness, I was prepared for the crushing grief that came with her loss. What blindsided me was the blessed relief that swept over me once her two-year, agonizing battle with ovarian cancer was over. The constant drain on our physical, emotional, and financial resources had finally come to an end.

I knew in my heart—and the letters Joanie left behind for me affirmed it—I would pick up the pieces. I would heal. My life would go on.

There was no such reprieve for Janice Bernstein. She had been braced for her husband's death, but learning that Cal had murdered a much-admired and respected doctor had thrown her into a deeper downward spiral.

I didn't think it was possible, but she looked even more haggard than when we met her two days ago. She was waiting for us on a bench near Mulvey's desk, and she stood up as soon as she saw me and Terry walk through the door.

Her eyes were red, and she spoke haltingly. "Can we talk in private?" she asked.

We took her to a quiet interview room, got her a cup of hot tea, and asked how we could help.

"I owe you an apology," she said. "Especially you, Detective Biggs. I hated you for even suggesting that my husband would kill a man for money, but now I think you could be right."

Terry and I sat there solemnly. She didn't need tough cop questions or soothing words of comfort. She needed someone to listen.

"Yesterday afternoon I got a call from a man who said his name was Mr. Welcome. He had a Caribbean accent, and when he told me he was with a bank in the Cayman Islands, and they had a half a million dollars in my name, I immediately thought it was a hoax, and I hung up.

"A minute later he called back. I recognized the Caller ID. Now I was angry. I picked up the phone, but before I could say anything, he said, 'Mickey and Minnie got married.' I started crying. That was the secret family password Cal and I taught the kids when they were little. We sat them down and said, 'If anybody ever tells you that Mommy and Daddy told them to pick you up and bring you home, ask them the password. If they don't know it, don't go with them, and talk to a policeman or a grownup you trust.' There was only one way Mr. Welcome could have known it. He was delivering a message from Cal."

Her eyes were watery, and she wiped away the tears. But not the pain. She buried her face in her hands. We waited till she could speak.

"He was very polite. He said that the account was opened with fifty thousand dollars a month ago. Cal told him to expect another four hundred and fifty thousand and asked him to call me when that was wired to the account. He warned Mr. Welcome that I wouldn't trust him, but the Mickey and Minnie password would help convince me it was real.

"I still had trouble believing it, so I called my sister-in-law who's a lawyer. She told me to have the bank wire twenty-five thousand dollars to my account here in LA. If it were a scam they wouldn't send a nickel, but Mr. Welcome said he would be happy to oblige. Ten minutes later I checked with my bank in Van Nuys. The money was deposited in my account, and I could draw on it immediately."

"Where do you think the money came from?" I asked.

"I don't know, but the only thing I can think of is what you suggested. Someone paid Cal to shoot the doctor. It's blood money. I don't want it. I don't want any part of it."

"Did your husband ever even hint that you'd be coming into a half a million dollars after he died?"

"No. He knew better than to tell me anything. I'd have asked him where the money was coming from, and I'd have pried the truth out of him. And then, I would never have let him do it."

I looked at Terry, and he nodded. I'm sure our minds were on the same track. Bruce Bower not only told his wife he was hired to kill Wade Yancy, he made her an accomplice. She paid for it with a bullet to the brain.

Cal Bernstein kept Janice completely in the dark, and that probably saved her life.

CHAPTER 29

TERRY AND I had no proof that Charlie Brock was our shooter, but he was far and away the leading candidate. We decided to extend an invitation to Mr. Brock for a sit-down chat, this time minus the beer and the camaraderie.

There was only one small problem.

"I can't find the fucker," Muller said.

"How is that possible?" Terry said. "He *lives* in LA. He *drives* a car."

"Thank you, Detective," Muller said. "How stupid of me not to check tax rolls, voter registration, or DMV records."

"He's got liver cancer," I said. "Does that help?"

"In a convoluted way, it just might," Muller said. "But it's going to take a while. I have to navigate my way around those pesky medical privacy laws."

While Muller tried to track down Charlie Brock, Terry and I set about unburying ourselves from a mountain of paperwork. The shooting on Homedale Street alone took a big chunk of the day, including a field trip back to the scene of the crime.

At 2 p.m. we got a hallelujah call from Eli confirming that the golf club we found in Bruce Bower's garage was a perfect match for the wedge-shaped divot in Wade Yancy's skull.

At 4 p.m. I was ready to haul ass and stick Terry with three more hours of grunt work. I had something more important to do than placate the LAPD paper bureaucracy. I was meeting Sophie and the family at LAX to celebrate the return of Carly Tan to America.

I was about to leave when my progress was impeded by an urgent call from my trusted informer at the front desk. "Melvis has entered the building," Officer Mulvey announced.

Deputy Mayor Mel Berger has many nicknames. Melvis is among the more flattering.

Most politicians prefer to oversee their domains from on high, but he has the annoying habit of showing up in the trenches unannounced in search of a progress report that is unsanitized and unfiltered. Half a minute after Mulvey's warning, Terry and I were summoned into Kilcullen's office to update Berger on the murder of the doctor who made the mayor a grandfather three times over.

He listened intently and didn't interrupt until we dropped the bomb about Wade Yancy. "And you're sure they're connected?" he asked.

"Positive," Terry said. "What we don't know is who's behind it all and who their next target might be."

Melvis glared at Terry as if he were the perp instead of the messenger. "Do you realize that a serial killer running around this city would be a disaster?"

"Actually, another six-point-seven quake like the one that hit Northridge would be a disaster," Terry said. "A serial killer would be more on the order of a media shitstorm that would land in your lap, but your point is well taken."

Terry is one of the few people in the department who can bust the deputy mayor's balls and get away with it. They have a history of mutual respect tempered by cautious uneasiness.

After we'd taken Berger through it all, he peppered us with many of the same questions we were still asking ourselves.

The meeting cost me fifty-three precious rush-hour traffic minutes, and I dashed out the door knowing I didn't have a prayer of getting to LAX before Carly's plane landed.

I called Diana from the road. "If I'm lucky," I said, "I'll get there before Carly clears customs. But just in case, take plenty of pictures. I don't want to miss the look on Sophie's face when she finally sees her mom after five months."

I'd have liked to go Code 3—lights and sirens all the way—but I'd rather be late than lose my job. Too many department vehicles wind up in wrecks even when they're legitimately violating the rules, so I resigned myself to the fact that I was just another citizen doing the speed limit, stopping at red lights, and avoiding the dangers of texting and driving.

It was slow going, and by the time I got to the airport and parked, Carly's plane had been on the ground for forty-five minutes. I hustled into the Tom Bradley International Terminal, and waded through a knot of people who were all on a similar mission when I heard an unmistakable voice bellow my name.

Big Jim was halfway across the terminal, holding Sophie's hand. As soon as she saw me, she pulled away and started running toward me, tears streaming down her cheeks. I knelt down and scooped her up in my arms.

"Don't let them take me away," she said.

"Sweetheart, don't worry. Nobody's taking you anywhere."

The rest of the welcoming committee—Big Jim, Angel, Diana, Frankie, and Izzy—converged on us.

"We got trouble, bro," Frankie said.

"We can handle it," I said. "I just need one of you—I repeat, *one* of you—to tell me what's going on. Diana, you talk. The rest of you, keep it zipped."

"Carly wasn't on the plane," Diana said. "She didn't text us, or warn us in advance, and at first we thought we had the wrong flight. Then two people came out of customs, saw the signs we had for Carly, and said they're her aunt and uncle."

She pointed at a Chinese couple in their mid- to late sixties who were standing quietly twenty feet away.

"They said Carly was arrested yesterday."

"Arrested? For what?"

"Political dissidence," Big Jim spat out, ignoring my ground rules.

"That doesn't even make any sense."

"It's China, Mike. It doesn't have to make sense."

"Are we sure that's Carly's aunt and uncle?" I said to Diana.

"I checked their passports," Big Jim said. "They also had a bunch of pictures on the cell phones—family shots with Carly. They're who they say they are, and don't get me wrong—they seem to be very nice people, and they genuinely want to help."

"I don't understand," I said. "If they want to help, why didn't they *call* us? Why did they fly halfway around the world to give us the bad news in an airport?"

"Damn it, Mike," Big Jim said. "They—"

"Stop!" Diana said, holding up her hand. "I'll tell him."

Angel added her vote, using her elbow to give Big Jim a nudge that was more like a body blow. He backed off.

"The aunt and uncle didn't come here to give us the bad news," Diana said, her eyes watery. "They came here for Sophie. They want to take her back to Beijing."

The little girl in my arms tightened her grip around my neck and started sobbing into my shoulder.

CHAPTER 30

BIG JIM WAS right. Daniel and Lucy Zhang were very nice people, and they definitely wanted to help. I just wasn't clear on what they came to help us with.

Angel, Frankie, and Izzy took Sophie to the food court, so that Big Jim, Diana, and I could find out.

The Zhangs had spent more than forty years working for a translation service company in Beijing, so it turned out that they spoke better English than any of us.

"I realize that this all comes as shock," Daniel said. "We considered trying to get a message to you, but the Chinese government has eyes and ears everywhere."

"We decided it was safer and wiser for us to fly to the states," Lucy said. "We do it often enough for business, so leaving the country wasn't an issue."

"My father told me that Carly was arrested for being a dissident," I said. "I find that incomprehensible. She's a nurse. She works with Diana at Valley General Hospital. And she's a naturalized American citizen."

"She's also an outspoken activist against human trafficking," Daniel said. "She was arrested several times in Beijing during her university days, but that was before the Jasmine Revolution of 2011. The penalties for inciting subversion are much more severe now."

"*Inciting subversion*?" Diana repeated.

"Not on the streets," Lucy said. "On the Internet. Are you aware of her blog?"

I turned to Diana, who looked just as dumbfounded as I was.

"Carly met Jeremy Tan and moved to LA about ten years ago. The government followed her blog, but their tentacles can only reach so far." Daniel said. "When Xiaoling became ill, Carly managed to get into the country without being noticed. But she couldn't stop posting, and when the electronic spy stations realized she was uploading her leftist rants from China, they tracked her down. She was planning her trip home when they arrested her."

"So she wrote a few critical blogs," Diana said. "How long can you lock someone up for that?"

Daniel lowered his head, reluctant to answer.

"It doesn't matter," Diana said. "Mike and I have taken care of Sophie for five months. We'll be happy to keep at it until Carly gets out of jail."

"She's not in jail," Lucy said softly. "She's in prison. She's been sentenced to twelve years."

I had my arm around Diana, and I felt her buckle when she heard the news. "That's not possible," she said.

"Not in America, perhaps," Lucy said. "But life is different in China."

"Excuse me," Big Jim said. "But I have a question."

"Of course," Daniel said.

"The truth is, I already know the answer," Big Jim said, "but I think Diana needs to hear it."

"Dad, just ask the question," I said.

"If you take Sophie back to China with you, how often will she get to spend quality time with her mother?"

"Carly is an enemy of the state," Daniel said. "She'll be in a forced-labor camp. Children are not welcome."

"Then why do you want to take this kid back to China?"

"That is a much less painful question to answer," he said, his eyes scanning the terminal, looking left, right, up, down, and then slowly making a second, even more deliberate pass.

"But you're not comfortable answering it here," I said.

He smiled. "No, I am not, Detective Lomax."

"Mike," I said.

"Mike," he said, nodding graciously. "Lucy and I are children of the Mao era. We have lived through war, famine, and the wholesale execution of forty-five million people at the hands of the greatest mass murderer in the history of the world. But unlike our niece, we won't sit in Starbuck's sipping cappuccino and churning out anti-government manifestos. If there's one thing we've learned after sixty-eight years of non-stop paranoia, it's to avoid having private conversations in public places."

"In that case," Big Jim chimed in, "I've got a twenty-eight-foot soundproofed Lincoln Town Car waiting right outside for you."

"Dad," I snapped, "we're not finishing this discussion in the back of a limo."

"Of course we're not," he said, picking up the Zhangs's luggage. "We're moving the party to your place. I'm just giving these nice folks a ride."

CHAPTER 31

EVEN ON A normal day Sophie asks too many questions, and this day was anything but normal. As soon as the four-foot-high sponge buckled up her seat belt, I turned to Diana, took in a deep breath, and exhaled a look that said, *Brace yourself for the inquisition.*

"What's political dissidence?" the sponge asked, getting the word right, even though she'd only heard it once.

Diana and I did our best to answer honestly, but still spare her the nightmare-inducing details like forced-labor camps, twelve years of confinement, and no visitation rights.

"So let me get this straight," Sophie said after draining us dry for most of the ride home. "My mother is an American, she went to China to be with *her* mother, and the Chinese government put her in jail for writing the thoughts that were in her heart."

"That's the gist of it," I said.

"Then why would you send *me* to China? I'm American, I want to be with my mother, and I write all kinds of thoughts," she said, challenging us with her watertight logic.

"You're not going to China," Diana said.

"You promise?"

We both promised. I didn't know if it was a promise we could keep, but I knew it was one Sophie needed to hear.

Having picked our brains and our souls clean, Sophie turned

on her iPod, plugged in her earbuds, and tuned out the world for the rest of the ride.

Frankie and Izzy had gone on ahead so that dinner would be ready by the time Sophie got home.

"I'm not eating party food," she said, passing up the Big Ugly Food Truck's *Almost Famous Pulled Pork And Melted Cheese Panini*. She went to the kitchen, made herself a peanut butter sandwich, and retired to her room to write, while the rest of us sat down with Daniel and Lucy Zhang to decide on her future.

"Daniel," I said, "Carly is an American citizen. Is there anything our government can do to convince your government to lighten her sentence?"

"You can make it a *cause célèbre*," he said. "I'm sure you can find journalists who could focus national—even worldwide—attention on the case. But in the end, China will not budge, and all you will have done is underscore the fact that Sophie's birth mother is incarcerated for the remainder of her childhood, and she's living with strangers who are no more than temporary legal guardians. Do you know what will happen when that news gets out, Mike?"

I knew. I looked around the room. We all knew. "Jeremy Tan will come after his daughter," I said.

"He has every right," Daniel said.

"He gave up that right," Diana said. "He abandoned her when she was six months old."

"I understand your outrage, Diana, but he didn't abandon her. He left Sophie in the care of her mother, and now that he's her only available biological parent, the courts won't rule against him."

"But at least if Jeremy got custody of Sophie, she could stay in America," I said. "That's what she wants."

"But it's not what Carly wants," Daniel said. "We were granted five minutes with her before she was taken away. As much as she hates uprooting her daughter, she believes that Sophie will fare better with us than she will with Jeremy. For one thing, he can't afford the private-school education Carly has been providing for her. We could match that in China."

"Mike and I can afford to send her to private school," Diana said. "How would Carly feel if we adopted her? Instead of being temporary guardians, we could make it permanent."

"I'm sure Carly would be thrilled," Lucy said, "but she is already embarrassed that she asked you to watch over Sophie for a few weeks, and it has turned into five months."

"Embarrassed? I'm sure that Mike will agree that it's been the best five months of our lives. I know Sophie would be happy with us. Just ask her."

"I think we would all be happier if she could stay here with you rather than being raised by a couple in their seventies in a foreign country," Lucy said. "But Sophie doesn't get a vote. None of us do. Only Jeremy can decide to waive his rights as a parent and allow you to adopt, and I doubt if he will."

"You don't know unless you ask," Big Jim said. "Let me talk to him."

A chorus of voices shouted no.

"I know you mean well," Daniel said, "but the last thing we want to do is alert Jeremy to the situation."

"So basically," Big Jim said, "you want to kidnap Sophie—smuggle her out of the country before her father finds out that she's up for grabs."

"Dad!" I said, slamming my hand against the arm of my chair.

"That's okay, Detective," Daniel said. "Lucy and I expected that emotions would run high. For the record, we are not kidnapping her. Not as long as we have written consent."

"From Jeremy?" Diana asked.

"No. From you and Mike. You're her legal guardians. As long as you give us a notarized letter of authorization giving us permission to take Sophie to China, none of us would be breaking any laws."

"Even if we know you're never going to bring her back?" Diana said.

"We wouldn't have to bring her back unless Jeremy got a US court order demanding that she be returned."

Big Jim stood up. "And that's when you'll start breaking the law," he said.

"Jim!" This time it was Angel. She rarely gets vocal when my father gets out of line, but when she does, he backs off.

"You'll have to forgive my husband," she said. "We've all come to love Sophie so much. This is a sad day for our family."

"Sorry," Big Jim mumbled.

"I think we all could use a break," Frankie said. "How about you all come out to the food truck and get something to eat?"

One by one they filtered out until only Diana and I were left in the room.

"What's going on?" she said.

"What do you mean?"

"I mean there's an eight-year-old girl who effectively just lost her mother and is faced with two horrible choices. Live with strangers in a strange land, or live with a father who hasn't paid any attention to her for her entire life. I felt like Big Jim and I were the only ones trying to come up with a better option."

"I know, but do me a favor," I said. "Next time you decide to adopt a kid, consult with me before you make the offer."

"I didn't think I had to."

"I don't know if Jeremy would even consider letting it happen, but right now I could use a little time before I pull the trigger on a major life-changing decision."

"I'm sorry," she said. "I just thought that given how serious the situation is, you wouldn't even have to think about it. How much time do you need?"

Ever since I left Doug Heller's office I had kept all my fears, my pain, and my anger bottled up inside. But Diana's question, innocent as it was, unleashed the demons.

"Dammit, Diana, babysitting for Sophie was a no-brainer, but asking me to take on the physical, emotional, and financial responsibilities of raising her is not something I can figure out over a pulled pork sandwich and a beer. I don't know how much time I need!"

I'd never lashed out at her like that before, and I could see the shock and the hurt in her eyes. But I wasn't ready to tell her the truth.

I didn't know how much time I had.

CHAPTER 32

WHEN CHARLIE BROCK first saw Dahlia Ben Ezra at a Living With Dying meeting he figured he'd already died and gone to heaven.

In a city full of cookie-cutter blondes with stars in their eyes and silicone in their chests, Dahlia was a raven-haired, dark-eyed natural beauty with the lithe body of a cat burglar. *And totally out of my league*, he thought.

But he was wrong. They had a lot more in common than a ticking clock. Dahlia was a former Israeli Air Force pilot who had flown air strikes over Lebanon and Syria, and Charlie had seen action with the US Marines in Afghanistan and Iraq.

The first night Dahlia joined the after-the-meeting drinking crowd at Halligan's, the chemistry between them crackled, and after one drink they broke off from the group and traded war stories. Three drinks later, he leaned across the table and asked if she could help him with a personal dilemma.

"My father and three of my uncles are rabbis," she said. "Personal dilemmas are my specialty."

"My doctor says I've got about a year," Charlie confided, "and in keeping with the spirit of this living with dying shit, I'd like to share that time with someone I can care deeply about."

"Do you have anyone in mind?" she asked.

"That's the dilemma. I kind of have my eye on two women,

but there are plusses and minuses to both."

"This is getting interesting. Tell me about them."

"The first one is reasonably good-looking. She has a solid job working for a company that sells marine insurance, and she's a loving family person—she's the sole provider for two aunts who are in their eighties. Every Sunday she takes them to mass and then out for lunch. She also volunteers at the church soup kitchen two mornings a week. She loves the arts, and her biggest passion is ballet. She often goes at the last minute and buys Standing Room Only tickets because she can't afford the price of a subscription."

"She sounds wonderful," Dahlia said. "What are her minuses?"

"Those *are* her minuses," Charlie said. "On the plus side, if I spend a year with her, it'll be the longest year of my life."

Dahlia shrieked with laughter. "I'm almost afraid to ask. What's your second option?"

"She captivated me the instant I saw her. She's exotic, hauntingly beautiful, mysterious, smart, funny, sexy—"

"I'm hoping those are plusses," Dahlia said. "What's the downside?

"I'm afraid that if I get involved with her, the last year of my life will fly by in a flash."

"The question is," she said, "do you want to live long, or do you want to live life?"

That night they became lovers. The next morning, they became business partners. Six weeks later, Dahlia Ben Ezra murdered a woman in Joshua Tree National Park.

Twenty-four hours after that she confirmed that a half a million dollars had been secured in her offshore account. "So what do you get out of this?" she asked, as she and Charlie lay in bed, naked and still entwined.

"I got you."

"Bullshit," she said. "You're no different from me. You'd sell your loyalty to the highest bidder."

"Okay, so my title is Head of Human Resources. I recruit, train, and interact with all the temporary help. And for that, I got a shitload of money to make sure my brother Kenny gets private care for the rest of his life."

"Not that it makes a difference," she said, "but I'm curious. Who's paying the freight for all this?"

"I have no idea. All the instructions I get are electronic. The only thing I know for sure is that it's someone with deep pockets and a major hard-on for Chilton-Winslow."

"It's probably another drug company," she said. "Or a Mexican cartel."

He laughed. "Did anyone ever tell you that you think like an Israeli?"

She rolled over and straddled him. "Is that a plus or a minus?"

He grabbed her ass and began moving slowly, rhythmically beneath her. With Dahlia there were no minuses.

They had decided they were both too fiercely independent to live together.

"But if we did, it might be fun to see which one of us kills the other one first," Dahlia said.

"I already know the answer, which is why I'm staying in my apartment where I know I'll wake up in the morning with all my body parts still attached."

And then one night Charlie showed up with two duffel bags and a laptop. "Sorry to fuck up what we've got," he said, "but I need a place to hide."

"From who?"

Dahlia reeled when Charlie told her the news. "You killed Bruce? *And* his wife? Why?"

"The cops were hauling them off to jail," Charlie said.

"Cops?"

"The same two dickheads who showed up at the meeting last night and grilled us about Cal. You're lucky you weren't there."

"Oh yeah, lucky for me I was hunched over a toilet bowl last night reminiscing about another memorable chemo session," she said. "All right, I can understand why you killed Bruce, but his wife didn't know anything."

"Her name was Claire, and she knew everything."

Dahlia's dark eyes opened wide. "What do you mean *everything*?" she asked.

"I mean Bruce told her all of it. He even took her on the job with him. She was in the car when he ran down Yancy."

"*He took her with him*? What happened to rule number one—don't tell a soul?"

"That's the problem with hiring amateurs, Dahlia. They don't always follow the rules."

"Even so, why would the cops arrest him? The accident report was cut and dried. Yancy was hit by a car. End of story."

"A car and a golf club," Charlie said. "Apparently Yancy didn't die fast enough, the wife called 911, and Bruce panicked. Bashed in his skull with the first thing he could find in his trunk. The medical examiner decided it didn't look like an accident."

"So Bruce broke rule number two, and the cartel, or whoever the hell they are, told you to kill him and his wife."

"They didn't tell me. I made the call on my own."

"Which means now they'll probably send someone to kill you."

"Just the opposite. I got a message this afternoon. They want to escalate."

"What does that mean?"

"The cops will start connecting the dead bodies. They know about Kraus and Yancy, and it won't take long for them to decide that Carolyn Butler had help falling off that mountain in Joshua Tree. Then they'll figure out who else might possibly be on the hit list and warn them. Our job is to kill off as many as we can as fast as we can, before they all go underground."

"At a half a million dollars a pop?"

"That's still the going rate."

Dahlia wrapped her arms around his neck and whispered in his ear. "You realize that this makes you the best boyfriend I ever had."

CHAPTER 33

TERRY WAS ON the phone when I got to the office Friday morning. "We're on our way," he said. "And doc... don't sedate him. We need him conscious."

"Sounds like Bruce is awake," I said as soon as he hung up.

"Claire wasn't that lucky," he said. "She died during the night."

"Have they told him yet?"

"No. Guess who gets to break the news to him."

I didn't have to guess.

"I know Bruce ran down Yancy intentionally," Terry said as we walked to the car, "but the poor bastard was desperate, and someone convinced him that if he did it they would take care of his wife after he was dead. Then they shot her through the head. They didn't even have the decency to wait for him to die."

Terry is one of those cops—tough on the outside, but he's always had a soft spot for the underdog, even in a case like this when he knew the underdog was a cold-blooded killer.

"Let's change the subject," he said, starting the car. "How did Sophie's reunion with her mom go?"

"Ugly."

He killed the engine and looked at me.

"Carly is in a Chinese prison for the next twelve years, and her family is trying to relocate Sophie to Beijing so that Jeremy Tan can't get custody."

"You're serious," he said.

"As a bullet through the brain."

I gave him the shorthand version of last night's drama. He asked a lot of the same questions Big Jim, Diana, and I had asked, but there were still no answers.

"You've got to fight it, Mike," he said. "It doesn't matter. Whatever you have to do. You can't let Sophie—"

And then he remembered. "Shit," he said. "You're still waiting on that lab report."

"At least you know why I'm not ready to storm into a lawyer's office and make a case for why I'm the best possible man to watch over Sophie for the next ten years."

"You are, Mike, and you're going to be around for a long time."

"I know this is going to sound like an asshole thing to say, but that's probably what Bruce Bower said to Claire."

He started the car, and we drove to the hospital in silence.

Bruce was in a private ICU suite, a uniformed cop sitting outside his door.

"He knows about his wife," she said.

"How did that happen?" Terry said.

"He kept asking for her, and one of the residents told him."

We thanked her and went inside.

Bruce's body was hooked up to a series of tubes that allowed fluids to drip in or drain out, and he was plugged into a tower of flashing, chirping, and beeping machines that monitored his vital signs like the black box on a Boeing 747. For a man who had just survived a shooting, only to wake up and remember he was still dying, he looked relatively alive. Not exactly rosy-cheeked, but not deathbed gray either.

"We're sorry for your loss," I said.

"It's my fault she's dead," he said, staring at the ceiling.

"No, it's not," Terry said. "Your friends betrayed you."

"They weren't friends. They hired me to kill Yancy and take the secret to my grave. I made the mistake of sharing it with

Claire. Did you get who killed her?"

"Not yet," Terry said. "Do you want to help us find him?"

No answer.

"Fine," Terry said, "but off the record, I'd have probably done exactly what you did."

"What's that supposed to mean?" Bower said, his eyes still glued to the ceiling.

"It means I'm not just a cop. I have a wife and three daughters, and if I were in your shoes—well, let's just say I understand why you did what you did. What I don't understand is why you won't let me and my partner get you the one thing you can't get for yourself."

"What's that?"

"Look at me, asshole!" Terry snapped.

Bower shifted in his bed and locked eyes with Terry. "My wife is dead, and I've got nothing left to live for. What the fuck could you possible get for me that I give a shit about?"

Terry lowered his voice to a whisper. "Payback."

CHAPTER 34

WITH THAT SINGLE word, Terry had given Bruce something to live for. We helped him sit up in his bed, and just to cover our asses, I reminded him of his Miranda rights. He gave me a sardonic smile when I said, "You have the right to remain silent."

"I'll be silent soon enough," he said. "What do you want to know?"

"Whatever you can give us," Terry said. "Just tell it in your own words."

"It was Labor Day," Bruce said. "I was still feeling pretty good back then, so Claire and I threw a little barbeque—invited half a dozen people from the program. We're all having a good time, and at one point Charlie pulls me aside and tells me about this company that's been doing clinical trials for a new cancer drug in Sweden. He says the results are phenomenal—even in Stage IV, but the FDA won't let them run any trials in the US.

"I tell him I'm not going to Sweden, and he tells me they're doing underground testing in LA. He says I'm the prefect candidate, and he can hook me up. But it's all super hush-hush. Don't tell Claire. Don't tell anyone.

"I figure what have I got to lose, so the next night Charlie picks me up, and he tells me there are some crazy ground rules. The company is so paranoid about getting caught that he's got to blindfold me so I don't know where their testing facility is. It's all starting to sound pretty hinky, and if it were anyone else I'd have bailed out. But it's Charlie, so I get in the back of his car, put on the blindfold, and I go along for the ride.

"It took maybe twenty minutes. I wish now that I'd paid more attention, but I just sat back and listened to music till we got there. Charlie walked me into the lobby of a building, still blindfolded. We took an elevator, maybe three or four floors, and he led me into a room, and said he would wait for me.

"The door closed, and a voice says I can take off my blindfold. I do, and I'm looking at myself in a mirror. I figured after all that undisclosed location bullshit it was probably one of those two-way mirrors where whosever on the other side can see you, but you can't see them. And then the voice thanks me for coming."

"Male or female?" I asked.

"It was filtered through one of those electronic synthesizers, like one of those phone robot voices. He, she, it said, 'You're not going to like what I'm about to tell you. Charlie lied. There are no clinical trials. There is no new miracle drug. There is no cure.'

"I'll never forget it. I'm staring at myself in the mirror, and I'm devastated. I finally say, 'If there's no cure, what the hell am I doing here?' And the voice says 'Claire is going to need money when you die. We're prepared to deposit half a million dollars in an offshore account in her name.' I say, 'What do I have to do for that? Kill someone?' The answer comes back, 'Precisely.' I go, 'Do I look like a hit man? I'm a fucking accountant.' And he says, 'But you have what we need, Bruce. You're going to be dead soon, and dead men are excellent at keeping secrets.'

"By now I'm freaking out. I get up and try to leave, but the door is locked. There's a pitcher of water there, and he tells me to pour myself a glass and calm down, but I'm not drinking anything this whack job puts in front of me. I know I'm locked in, so I try to humor him. I tell him I need the money, but I can't kill anyone. He says, 'Let me see if I can change your mind.'

"He asked if I ever heard of Chilton-Winslow. I had. He says that their most lucrative product is this hormone shot that women get if they're having trouble conceiving. It helps her produce more eggs, then the docs harvest them and use the best ones for in vitro fertilization.

"Five years ago Chilton figured out how to make the same drug for two-thirds less than the real thing. When they tested it, they found out that the new formula worked even better than the old one. So not only were they making more money per dose, but more women got pregnant, so more doctors started using it, and the upside for the company was in the billions.

"There was only one problem. The tests showed that some of the women were getting sick with the new stuff. Not just sick—dying. By all rights Chilton should have pulled it off the market. But they don't. A handful of people at the top of the food chain decide to bury the test results and keep the product on the market. Wade Yancy was one of them. His job was to sell as much of that poison as possible until the FDA woke up and said, 'Hey guys, you have a problem.'"

Bower closed his eyes, no doubt reliving that night in his head.

"I'm sorry," he said, his eyes opening. "I'm not doing the story justice. He gave me plenty of facts, figures—all kinds of details that convinced me this wasn't bullshit. By the time he was done I figured, hell, somebody should kill this bastard. For half a million bucks, it might as well be me."

My heart was pounding. "Do you remember the name of the fertility drug?" I asked.

"Ovamax. And it's still on the market. According to the mystery voice, there are at least seventy-three cases of women who took the shots hoping to have a baby, but wound up dying of ovarian cancer instead."

I felt my knees buckle. Joanie had been one of them.

CHAPTER 35

I HAD TO leave the room. Terry followed me.

"What just happened?" he said. "I thought you were going to pass out."

"Joanie was on Ovamax," I said. "One injection a day for two weeks. She hated giving herself needles, so I had to do it. She used to joke about it. Once she called the station and left a message with Mulvey—'Tell Detective Lomax to come home and shoot his wife.'"

"Sounds like Joanie," Terry said, an appreciative grin spreading across his face

"We tried it for three separate cycles, so I probably pumped that toxic shit into her body about forty times." I covered my face with one hand and dug my nails into my scalp. "Fuck!"

"You want me to finish the interview?" Terry said.

I pulled my hand away. "No. I want to find out who paid to have Yancy and Kraus killed, and then I want to be locked in a room with them until they give me the names of everyone involved in the cover-up at Chilton-Winslow."

"And then what?" Terry said. "Hunt them down and kill them yourself? No one would ever suspect you."

"Kiss my ass, Biggs."

"Attaboy. Now you're starting to sound like your old self again. Let me ask you something, Lomax. Does it come as a surprise to you that a giant corporation put profits over humanity? The big banks do it, the oil companies do it, hell, they all do it. I have no trouble believing that Chilton-Winslow covered up the truth so they could add a few billion dollars to their bottom line. But all that means is *they* killed Joanie. Not you."

"I know," I said.

"So let's go back and see what else we can get out of Bruce, because this case just got personal. As of now, he's not the only one looking for payback."

We went back in, and Terry took the lead. "Tell us what happened after you agreed to kill Yancy."

"This faceless voice gave me the rules. They were pretty simple. Make it look like an accident, and don't tell anyone, not even your wife. But I couldn't keep it from Claire. She was worried sick about money. I had a solid plan for our golden years, but I never planned on dying at fifty-one, and Claire was positive that I'd die broke, and she'd wind up homeless. I kept telling her she'd be okay, but she didn't believe me, so I finally showed her the Cayman Islands bank account. There was already fifty thousand in it. I explained what I had to do to earn the rest, and once I told her, she said she didn't want me to be alone. She wanted to come with me. If I'd have played by the rules, she'd still be alive."

"Cal Bernstein's wife told us you and he were friends," Terry said. "Did you know he was recruited?"

"Not at first, but we were having coffee one night after the meeting, and Cal somehow let on that his wife was going to be taken care of when he was dead. And I knew—I just knew. I said, 'Did Charlie blindfold you and take you for a ride? Did you talk to some ghost behind a two-way mirror?' And it was like two guys who are lost in the desert who find each other. You still may not know the way, but God, it's good to have company. We talked about how we were going to do it. Cal was in sporting goods. He knew a lot about guns."

"He didn't make it look an accident," I said.

"The plan was that he was going to bust in to Kraus's office like a junkie who was jonesing for drugs. He was going to shoot the doc and steal a script pad and whatever drugs he could grab in a hurry. It was supposed to look like a robbery gone bad. He didn't expect the cops to be there. I guess once you saw him, his whole crazy-junkie story blew up. So he killed himself."

"You say Charlie Brock recruited you," I said.

"He recruited Cal too. Those are the only ones I know, but I know they had a much bigger hit list. Charlie is probably still hanging around the LWD meeting looking for terminal assassins."

"He's not hanging around anywhere," Terry said. "Which makes us think he's the one who shot you and Claire. Do you know where he lives?"

"No. If I did, I'd pull out these tubes and be on the way to his house."

"You wouldn't get very far," Terry said. "You're still under arrest. There's a cop right outside your door."

"I know I'm going to jail, but do you think I can get permission to go to Claire's funeral?"

"I think that can be arranged," Terry said.

"Thanks. It's just going to be me, her brother, and maybe a few cousins. Claire and I never had kids. We tried, but it didn't take. Back then we didn't think we had a lot of options. Our lives might have been completely different if we had gone to a fertility doctor."

I looked at Terry, and I'm sure he knew what I was thinking. Joanie and I *had* gone to a fertility doctor. And our lives might have been completely different if we hadn't.

CHAPTER 36

WE LEFT UCLA Med and drove straight to City Hall. One of Mel Berger's other nicknames is Deputy Mayor in Charge of Dirty Little Secrets. His network of moles extends from Bel Air to Skid Row, from Sacramento to DC, from the stalls of the Farmers Market on Fairfax to the executive suites of the Fortune 500.

We told him what we'd learned from Bruce Bower.

"Do you believe him?" Berger said.

"Of course we believe him," Terry said. "Why would he lie? He wants to help us track down the people who killed his wife."

"I'm sure Bower *believes* he's telling you the truth," Berger said, "but have you considered that all he's doing is repeating the same bullshit story somebody behind a two-way mirror fed him in order to convince him to murder Wade Yancy?"

"It sounds like you've got your own version of the same story," Terry said.

Berger nodded. "I am well aware of the Ovamax debacle," he said. "I heard it firsthand from Egan Granville."

"And who is that?"

"Mr. Granville is a close personal friend of the mayor, a major fundraiser on our behalf, and the CEO of Chilton-Winslow Pharmaceuticals. I'm surprised you haven't heard of him, since his picture was on page nine of today's *LA Times*."

"It's been a busy morning," Terry said. "I haven't even had time to open the paper and check my horoscope. What was on page nine?"

"Granville was nominated by the President for a cabinet position—Secretary of Health and Human Services. I watched his Senate confirmation hearing on C-SPAN yesterday. He was asked about Ovamax, and he handled it quite well."

"Fill us in."

"Your Mr. Bower was right about the problem. About five years ago, Dr. Amanda Dunbar was the head of Research and Development for Chilton when she came up with an ingenious process for creating a synthesized version of clomiphene citrate, which the company marketed as Ovamax. Dr. Dunbar trumpeted it as more effective and more profitable. Chilton went with it, and when their fortunes multiplied, they in turn rewarded Dr. Dunbar handsomely. What she didn't tell them was that there was one devastating effect that had never manifested itself with the original formulation—the risk of ovarian cancer in infertile women increased tenfold.

"By the time the FDA became aware of it, a number of women had died. The company swore that they had no knowledge of it and quietly replaced the defective product with the earlier version. They also paid a fine."

"How much?" I said.

"I believe it was four hundred million dollars, which was substantially less than the money they earned while the other product was out there."

"Did anyone go to jail?"

"Dr. Dunbar was fired, and I know for a fact that the FDA is still investigating whether they can follow up with criminal charges, but so far they can't prove that she knew the risks."

"What about the women who died?" Terry said. "Did their families sue?"

"One did, but the case was thrown out. Like all patients, she had signed a waiver acknowledging that she understood and accepted the risks of taking the drug, and indemnifying the company and the physician from any and all adverse reactions."

"And I'm guessing the court considers death just another one of those pesky adverse reactions," Terry said.

"Detective, I'm only giving you Egan Granville's sworn testimony on what happened with Ovamax. A Senate confirmation committee bought it. If you choose not to—"

"Do *you*?"

"Do I take the word of one of the mayor's biggest supporters over that of a dying man who has just been arrested for first-degree murder? What do you think? Besides, my personal opinion is totally irrelevant. The only thing that matters in this job is who I stand with."

"I get it," Terry said. "You're a politician. Lomax and I are cops. You can buy into whatever story comes from the highest bidder. Mike and I have to follow up on every lead, and right now, the man who murdered Wade Yancy says there's an Ovamax hit list."

"If that's true," Berger said, "then I suggest you hurry up and check on the well-being of Dr. Dunbar. She's the one that all the fingers on both sides are pointing to."

"I haven't consulted with my partner yet," Terry said as the two of us headed toward the door, "but I'm pretty sure we both thought of that as soon as you mentioned her name. We're also going to pay a little visit to the mayor's friend, benefactor, and cabinet-member-to-be, Mr. Egan Granville."

Berger bristled. "Why would you want to talk to Granville? Do you think he knows anything more than he told the Senate committee? He's the CEO of a multi-billion-dollar global health care company. Take my advice, Detective Biggs, and do not harass him."

"Thank you for your counsel, Mr. Deputy Mayor," Terry said, standing in the doorway, poised to leave. "I may not be on board with everything you've put forth, but there is one thing you said that I agree with wholeheartedly."

"And what's that?"

"Your personal opinion is totally irrelevant."

CHAPTER 37

"YOU'VE GOT TO hand it to Mel Berger," Terry said once City Hall was in our rearview mirror. "Who else can give up details of the atrocities at Chilton-Winslow, and then casually label it all as 'the Ovamax debacle'?"

"The man is a brilliant spin doctor," I said.

"Speaking of evil doctors, I'm guessing this Dr. Amanda Dunbar who came up with the new formula is high on our vigilante's hit list. Can you give Muller a call and have him track her down before she becomes just another chalk outline and a name in red Sharpie on our white board?"

Despite the fact that I'd have liked to kill Dr. Dunbar myself, it was my job to warn her. I made the call to Muller.

Twenty minutes later Terry and I were on a quiet stretch of Bristol Parkway in Culver City. Brushed-nickel letters set in a thirty-foot span of stone announced that we had arrived at the West Coast Campus of Chilton-Winslow.

The building, a simple eight-story steel-and-glass affair, was unpretentious as LA architecture goes, but the perfectly sculpted topiary gardens that lined the driveway would have fit right in had we been visiting British royalty.

"Their landscaping budget alone could feed a small nation," Terry said. "But I'm sure their stockholders would agree it's money well spent."

We entered the lobby where a trio of blazer-clad rent-a-cops stood at an imposing marble desk.

"LAPD," I said, flashing tin. "We're here to talk to Egan Granville."

The two guards at either end quickly deferred to the one in the center. His name tag read Eddie Montalvo. "Is Mr. Granville expecting you?" he asked, reaching for a phone.

I blocked the reach. "Don't call. We want to surprise him."

"Mr. Granville is in Washington DC," Montalvo said. "I was calling Ms. McGirr."

"And who's that?"

"She's the wolf at the door. Nobody, but nobody, gets to see Mr. Granville lest Ms. McGirr puts them through. And let me tell you, Detective, she's not too keen on surprises."

"I guess the wolf is going to have to adapt," I said. "Lead the way."

Montalvo led us to an elevator marked Private, and used a key to access the eighth floor. The doors opened, and we stepped into a gallery of museum-quality art. Montalvo carded us through a thick glass door, then steered us to an imposing L-shaped desk.

A well-dressed woman in her late forties looked up. The name plate on her desk said Marion McGirr, and the look in her eye said, *Don't fuck with me*. Clearly she was not happy to see the three of us invading her space unannounced.

"Sorry to bust in without calling, Ms. McGirr," Montalvo said, "but these two gentlemen want to ask Mr. Granville some questions."

McGirr looked at me and Terry. "You and every other reporter in Los Angeles. You're wasting your time and mine. The Senate doesn't vote until Monday. We'll hold a press conference Monday afternoon. Have your editor contact our public relations people."

"We don't have an editor, but we do have these badges that say LAPD homicide," Terry said, extending his. "We're investigating the murder of Kristian Kraus, and we can't wait till Monday."

She stood up and checked his ID. Then she asked for mine. "Marion McGirr," she said once she was convinced she was stuck with us. She dismissed Montalvo with a single nod of her head.

"We were all stunned by the news of Dr. Kraus's murder," she said. "He was a major asset to our company. Mr. Granville has been in Washington DC since it happened. I'm not sure how he could possibly help you with your investigation, but I've been his personal assistant for twenty-three years. I assure you I can answer any questions on his behalf."

"I'm sure you can answer them all brilliantly," Terry said. "And yet the United States Senate insisted on interviewing him and not you. LAPD operates pretty much the same way. We prefer getting our answers straight from the horse's mouth. Perhaps you can tell us when the horse will be back in LA."

Terry is skilled at putting people in their place in a big hurry. Most of them resent him for it, and they usually turn to me, hoping I'm the designated good cop. Not Marion McGirr. Her job was to cut people off at the knees, and suddenly, without warning, she found herself on the receiving end of the cut.

Maybe there's an unwritten code among hard-asses, but instead of getting pissed off, McGirr let a half smile of admiration spread over her face. She had been bested by a master.

"Mr. Granville will be flying in with some of our senior officers Sunday morning. There's a board meeting at 2 p.m. It will be his last one. The Senate will vote on his nomination Monday, and at this point it appears it will be unanimous. Do you gentlemen work Sundays?"

"Yes ma'am," I said. "What time does he arrive?"

"The corporate jet lands at Van Nuys Airport at 9:30. They'll chopper over here. I can put you on his calendar for ten. Does that work?"

"It does," I said. "Thank you for your time. By the way, I read that one of your other executives was killed in a car accident. Sad times for your company. We're sorry for your loss."

"That was Wade Yancy. He was Vice President of Brand Development. We were just getting over his death when Dr. Kraus was taken from us. I guess what they say is true—bad things happen in threes."

"Threes?" I said.

"A few weeks prior to that another one of our senior people, Carolyn Butler, died in a climbing accident. Let's hope this is the end of it."

"Let's hope so," I said.

Based on Bruce Bower's testimony, the person behind the two-way mirror had a hit list. And now that the body count was up to three, I was starting to think we were more at the beginning than the end.

CHAPTER 38

AS SOON AS we left Chilton, I called Muller and added Carolyn Butler's climbing accident to his already full plate.

By the time we got back to the office the boy genius was ready for us.

"Carolyn Butler was scaling a four-hundred-foot vertical face at Joshua Tree National Park last month when her rope snapped, and she fell a hundred feet to her death," he said.

"Just like that?" Terry said. "Her rope snapped?"

"Climbing has its dark side," Muller said. "Apparently that's part of the rush."

"And it was deemed an accident?"

"Signed, sealed, and verified by the ME. Joshua Tree is over twelve hundred square miles, Detective. It wasn't the first accidental death, and it won't be the last. But they've never had a homicide—at least none that they know of."

"What did you find on Amanda Dunbar?" Terry said.

"Enough to send you and Lomax on an all-expense-paid trip along the Pacific Coast Highway, which is renowned for its scenic beauty and frequent landslides," Muller said, a hint of a smile on his farm-boy face. "Dr. Dunbar left Chilton with a considerable retirement package, bought a house on Cliffside Drive in Malibu, and has been there ever since."

"Let's pay her a visit," Terry said.

"One thing before you go," Muller said. "Take a look at these mug shots."

He laid out seven pictures on his desk. Terry and I both pointed our fingers at the same one. "That's Charlie Brock," he said.

"Really?" Muller said. He looked even more surprised than we were.

"Really," I said. "Who did you think it was?"

He flipped the picture over. "His real name is Peter Thatcher."

"How did you find him?"

"You said he had liver cancer, so I started searching the medical databases looking for a Charles Brock. I came up empty. So I had this thought: If I had a diseased organ, what would I want to do?"

"Try to get a healthy one," Terry said.

"Exactly. A transplant. So I called UCLA and got a list of all their transplant candidates for the last two years."

"You're a genius," I said.

"No, I'm an idiot, but luckily I'm married to a genius. Last night I was telling Anette what I was looking for, and she told me that Charlie wouldn't qualify for a new liver if the old one has cancer. I said, 'You'd think being married to a nurse I'd have known that.'"

"I live with a nurse, and I didn't know that," I said.

"Anette says a lot of people don't know that, so they apply, and they get rejected. I took a ride over to UCLA, pulled out the files of the liver transplant rejects that fit Charlie's description—white, male, forties—and I came up with this batch here." He held up the picture we fingered. "You sure this is him?"

"He's definitely the person we met at the Living With Dying meeting," Terry said, "but Mike and I won't know if he's the one who shot the Bowers until after we sit him down and ask him a few questions. Thanks a lot. Great job."

Terry started to walk towards the door, then stopped and turned around. "I almost forgot to ask," he said. "By any chance did your wife also happen to get this guy's address?"

CHAPTER 39

TWENTY MINUTES AFTER we zeroed in on Charlie Brock's real identity, Muller worked up a quick background and rattled off the bullet points for us.

"Peter Martin Thatcher, forty-seven, born Vallejo, California, attended UC Santa Barbara, majored in poli-sci, pulled six years with the Marines, two tours in the Gulf, honorable discharge, worked as a boat mechanic in Long Beach until five months ago, which coincides with the date he tried to get a new liver and was told, 'Sorry, Charlie.'"

"They probably said, 'Sorry, Peter,'" Terry volunteered.

Muller looked at me. "Does he ever let up?"

"Trust me, he's even worse when he doesn't talk," I said.

"Thatcher's been renting a furnished apartment on West Valley Boulevard in Alhambra," Muller said, handing me the address. "That's all I can give you right now."

"We've got guns and vests," Terry said, "so that's all we need. Thanks."

Terry and I drove to a two-story white stucco faux-hacienda rat trap that Thatcher/Brock called home. The building manager, a clueless, past-his-prime surfer dude who reeked of weed and apathy, gave us the key to what he referred to as Unit Four.

We drew our weapons, knocked on the door, and Terry bellowed out the mandatory "Open up, LAPD" salutation. Getting no response, and because the occupant was a bona fide suspect in a homicide investigation, we entered unencumbered by any further legal constraints that normally bog down our unrelenting quest for justice.

The apartment looked like it had been stormed by insurgents. The lone closet had been ransacked, and whatever clothes hadn't been strewn on the floor were spilling out of three open dresser drawers. A black plastic garbage bag was stuffed with crushed Budweiser cans, grease-stained Papa John's pizza boxes, and the rotting remains of rice, beans, and bones from El Pollo Loco.

"Looks like liver cancer boy is on a health kick," Terry said.

The entire apartment consisted of a single eighteen-by-twelve room with a tiny toilet in one corner. In the opposite corner was a black matte gun locker. Unlocked. Terry swung the door open. It was the only thing in the place that had been stripped clean.

"Good news for some anxious apartment hunter who's looking for something with that trendy Smith & Wesson flair," Terry announced. "Charlie Brock has clearly moved on. Unit Four is definitely on the market."

"Let's look around and see if he left a forwarding address," I said.

There were stacks of books that ran the length of one entire wall. We started on opposite ends.

"You've got to admire a killer who's read *The Art Of War*," Terry said, holding up a dog-eared copy of Sun Tzu's classic. "Plus the mind-fucking prose of Nietzsche, John Locke, Carl Jung, and the ever-enlightening Ayn Rand. What have you got over there?"

"I don't believe it," I said. "This weirdo has the entire collection of Nancy Drew mysteries."

Terry's head snapped around. "Son of a—" As soon as he saw the shit-eating grin on my face, he stopped. But it was too late. I'd nailed him. It was a rare moment.

His lovable ugly mug lit up, and he beamed. "Good one, grasshopper. Mr. Miyagi so proud."

"Step over here, sensei," I said. "I think I found what Nancy would refer to as a couple of real nifty clues."

There was a pile of Chilton-Winslow annual reports that dated back five years and a manila envelope thick with Internet printouts on Ovamax. In an ideal world, I'd have liked them to be front-page stories by Pulitzer-winning investigative reporters from the *LA Times*, but most of them were the rants of bloggers, conspiracy theorists, and Big Pharma haters.

I didn't care. As far as I was concerned, the source didn't matter. The verdict was unanimous. Ovamax caused ovarian cancer, and the greedy bitch behind it all was Dr. Amanda Dunbar.

Then we rifled through the pages of the annual reports, which had been highlighted for our convenience. The unconscionable sales and profit numbers had been underlined in black.

"Bingo," Terry said as we turned to a two-page photo spread of all the people who had helped catapult the company to success. Three of the faces had been X'd out in red. Carolyn Butler, Kristian Kraus, and Wade Yancy.

"Who do you think is next on their list?" Terry asked.

"I don't know, but let's start with Amanda Dunbar," I said. "It's time I met the woman who killed my wife."

CHAPTER 40

THE IRON GATE to Amanda Dunbar's Tuscan-style fortress clicked open, and Terry and I drove slowly up the winding driveway of one of the most well-guarded homes in Bel Air Crest, one of LA's most exclusive private communities.

Security cameras tracked us all the way, and a pair of gleaming-coated Dobermans stood under the portico watching our every move as we waited for a two-legged sentry to give us the green light to get out of our car.

"I have a feeling Dr. Dunbar may already suspect someone is out to kill her," Terry said.

A tall Asian man stepped out of the house, checked our IDs, and then silently escorted us to a sparsely furnished chrome-and-glass office, where Dunbar was waiting for us.

She was about forty, smaller than I expected—five feet at best, with a taut, trim body, capped by a thatch of copper hair in a no-nonsense pixie cut.

"This is about the Kristian Kraus shooting," she said. It was not a question.

"Yes, ma'am," Terry said.

"By now you realize he's not the only one," she said. "You've connected him to Wade Yancy and Carolyn Butler, or you wouldn't be here. If you came to warn me that I'm in the crosshairs, thank you, but I'm way ahead of you."

"Do you have any idea who might want to kill you?" Terry asked.

"Detective, there are a lot of people who lost loved ones because of Chilton-Winslow's greed. They despise the company and everyone connected to Ovamax. I'm high on their list, and I've got the hate mail to prove it."

"Can we see them?" Terry said.

She opened a desk drawer and pulled out a thick folder. "This is all the snail mail plus printouts of the emails I've gotten so far. Some of them are just rants, and some are so poignant, they can bring you to tears. But don't plan on arresting anyone, because none of them are out-and-out death threats—unless you count the dead mackerel that came wrapped in a copy of *L'Italo-Americano*."

Terry took the folder and thumbed through it. "I thought they'd be anonymous, but most of them are signed. Did you respond?"

"And say what? 'I'm sorry for your loss, but it's not my fault. I'm innocent.'"

"If you're so innocent," Terry said, "why are you getting dead fish?"

"I was the head of the R&D team that developed the new formulation. The early test results were spectacular. The new Ovamax cost less to make and it resulted in more pregnancies. Yancy and his team jumped all over it. They pumped hundreds of millions into marketing, teaming up with the best fertility docs in the business. The profits broke all company records, and top prescribers like Kraus got paid a fortune in what is affectionately known as *royalties*."

"It looks like you were pretty well compensated yourself," Terry said.

"I was, but two years into the gold rush I got some alarming new test results. Some of our patients developed ovarian cancer. Yancy immediately said there was no concrete proof that it was connected to us, and Carolyn Butler, our chief counsel, backed him up. She had our legal department bury disclaimers in all our printed material that she guaranteed would make us bulletproof. Then the docs were instructed not to administer Ovamax until the patient—and her spouse—signed ironclad liability waivers."

I remembered Joanie signing. I balked, but Kraus assured us it was a mere formality. "Just a bunch of lawyers covering their asses," he said. I signed.

"Money was pouring in, and nobody wanted to kill the golden goose," Dunbar said, "but the death toll kept going up. These women were in the prime of their lives, and the number of Ovamax patients getting sick and dying was six hundred percent greater than women not on the drug. I finally went to Granville and told him to either pull it off the market, or I'd blow the whistle.

"He agreed. They did a production run on the original formulation for a few weeks—long enough for me to believe it was done. Then they quietly went back to the deadlier, more profitable version. It was another two years before the FDA picked up on the rising number of deaths. Just before the whole thing hit the fan, Chilton offered me a deal. They would pull the product from the market and pay me a shitload of money if I resigned and signed a contract never to go public with the truth. So I took the fall."

"You took the fall and the money," I said.

"And I've got millions that I won't live to spend," she said.

"Meaning what?" I said.

"Meaning I had my own infertility problems, so I went to see Kristian Kraus, and he put me on Ovamax. I thought it was the original formulation, but by the time I realized they had all been lying, I had Stage III ovarian cancer." She removed her wig and stared at me defiantly.

"Do you know Charlie Brock? " I asked.

She glared at me. "Never heard of him."

"Peter Thatcher?"

"No."

"Bruce Bower?"

"No."

"Cal Bernstein?"

"Him I heard of. He made the eleven o'clock news for shooting Kristian Kraus. I didn't know him, but I'm guessing he was another dissatisfied Ovamax customer. There are a lot of them out there."

"Besides yourself," I said, "who else do you think is on their hit list?"

She held up her hand. "That's it, detectives. No more questions. You may give a rat's ass who's next, but leave me out of it."

She pressed a red button on her electronic alert bracelet. "If you want my opinion, here it is—the two of you are in way over your heads. You may know a thing or two about how to catch a killer, but you know nothing about the politics of Big Pharma, and even less about Granville and his medical Mafia. They would poison their own mothers to make a buck."

Our Asian escort and his two canine companions appeared in seconds.

"I know more than you think, Dr. Dunbar," I said as Terry and I walked toward the door. "My wife was one of the women they poisoned."

CHAPTER 41

DRIVING HOME I realized that Diana hadn't called me all day. Totally understandable. After the shabby way I treated her the night before, I deserved to be ignored. Of course, I hadn't called her either, but not because I was pissed. I'd behaved like a jerk, and it was easier to avoid her than to attempt to undo the damage over the phone.

I was ready to face the music when I saw Red Ryder parked in my driveway. That's what my father calls his 1949 Willys pick-up truck. He's got more than fifty movie rental cars and trucks in his stable, and since the painstakingly restored, fire engine red Willys was Sophie's favorite, it was easy to figure out why that was the one he drove to our house.

Sophie's biggest ally was here to plead her case. It was all I could do to keep from making a U-turn and finding the nearest bar.

Big Jim was waiting for me in the living room, nursing a beer. "Where are Sophie and Diana?" I asked.

"They went out for pizza with Angel. It's just you and me till they get back. Would you like something to drink? There's beer in the fridge."

I sat down. "I'll pass. What I *would* like is an explanation. Why am I being ambushed?"

"What do you mean ambushed?"

"You're waiting for me in *my* house, offering me *my* beer, and you've eliminated all possible witnesses. I don't know what you call it, but I'm calling it an ambush. What are you doing here?"

"What the hell do you *think* I'm doing here?"

"Meddling in my life. Prying into things that are none of your business. Sticking your nose where it doesn't belong. It's the same shit you've done to me ever since I was a kid, but this time around I have two words for you—back off."

"I'm not meddling," said the man who has no problem inflicting his opinion on people whether they ask for it or not. "Consider this an intervention."

"News flash, Dad—I know you're convinced that you've been put here on earth to help us mere mortals cope, but I don't want your help."

"That's what an intervention *is*, Mike. It's when you reach out to people in need when they're too dumb to ask for help on their own. Now, let's get down to the nitty-gritty. When was the last time you saw a doctor?"

That blindsided me. I'd seen more than my fair share of doctors in the past four days, but I thought I'd done a good job of keeping it on the down low. *What did Big Jim know?*

"What are you talking about?" I sputtered out. "What kind of a doctor?"

"A proctologist to help you get your head out of your ass, damn it! Sophie needs you. I thought you loved her. How in God's name can you let them take her away to China for the next twelve years? You may have to fight Jeremy for custody, but why the hell would you walk away from that little girl without putting up a fight?"

I stood up.

"Don't you walk out on me," he barked.

"My house, Jimbo. One of us will be walking out, and it won't be me."

I went to the kitchen, grabbed a bottle of Blue Moon, and took a calming swig. Big Jim had simply said the word *doctor*, and I went full-blown paranoid on him. It wasn't until he followed up with his lame proctologist joke that I realized he didn't know anything about my medical issues.

And that's the way it was going to stay until I had something concrete to share with him.

I went back to the living room, eased back into my chair, and took another hit on the beer. "Did Diana put you up to this?" I asked.

"That's not her style, and you know it," he said. "But I do happen to know that you came down pretty hard on her last night when she suggested that the two of you adopt Sophie. Angel caught her crying outside while the rest of us were eating dinner. Diana didn't give up much, but it was pretty clear to Angel what went on between the two of you."

"So Angel told you, and you decided to do what you do best, and fix my relationship with Diana."

"Give me a break, Mike. I'm not trying to fix anything. I'm only trying to help. What can I do?"

"You want to help?" I snapped. "Then why don't you do the one thing I've asked you to do and back the fuck off!"

"Back off? Jesus, Mike, we have a crisis on our hands. Sophie's mother has been locked up by one of the most repressive governments on the planet, and her father, who's been MIA most of her life and probably couldn't pick her out of a lineup, may try to lay claim to her. The kid is scared to go to sleep because she's afraid she'll wake up in fucking China, and you want me to back off?"

"So you *did* hear me," I said. "Thanks for the intervention, Dad. Now take your beer and hit the road. This is my problem. Mine and Diana's."

"You're not going to listen to Diana any more than you'll listen to me," he said, getting out of his chair. "I knew that before I came over, but I figured there's still one person who can talk sense to you."

"And who might that be?"

He took an envelope out of his pocket and handed it to me. "Joanie."

I looked at Joanie's familiar handwriting on the outside of the envelope. There was no question who it was from. "Where... where did you get this?"

"Joanie gave it to me a month before she died."

"That's impossible. She wrote nine letters. I have them all."

"She *gave* you nine letters, Mike. But she wrote a few more and gave them to me to give to you on special occasions. I haven't read any of them. I just know when I'm supposed to deliver them."

"And what special occasion is this?"

"Joanie was hoping that one day you'd get remarried, and your new wife would be pregnant, and you'd finally be about to have that baby she wasn't able to give you."

"This isn't that," I said.

"So shoot the messenger. As far as I'm concerned, whether you like it or not, you're on the cusp of fatherhood, and you're not sure which way to go. I figure maybe Joanie can help you make up your mind."

He walked out of the room and left the house. I sat there, unable to stand, a letter from my dead wife in my trembling hand.

CHAPTER 42

DIANA AND SOPHIE didn't get back till after nine. I yelled hello as they came through the door and got one hello back. Diana. I went into the kitchen where she was getting the coffee ready for the morning.

"Where's the kid?" I said.

"It's past her bedtime. I told her to wash up and brush her teeth in a hurry."

"Well she didn't waste any time saying hello. How was pizza with Angel?"

"Fun. How was your visit with Big Jim?"

"What's a dozen notches down from fun?"

"He's on a mission to get you to adopt Sophie. Angel and I both told him to give you some space."

"That's basically what I suggested. Except I may have used slightly different words."

I was hoping for a laugh, or at least a smile, but she gave me neither.

"Look, Diana, I'm sorry about jumping down your throat last night, but this whole thing with Carly caught me by surprise."

"It caught all of us by surprise—Sophie most of all. But you're a cop, Mike. I thought you could handle surprises."

"Did you hear the part where I apologized for last night?"

"I heard the part where you said, *I'm sorry, but*, and then you tried to blame your bad behavior on the bad news itself. Fine. I accept your apology, but I don't buy your explanation. The sudden shock of Carly's arrest is over. It's twenty-four hours later, and right now we're looking at a very harsh reality. Sophie can either move in with a father she doesn't know in LA, or an aunt and uncle she doesn't know in Beijing. The Mike Lomax I know would be scrambling to give the girl some better options. But you're not. I don't know what your problem is, but it has nothing to do with the bombshell Daniel and Lucy dropped on the family last night. By the way, they're picking her up in the morning."

"The morning? Bullshit. They can't take her out of the country without our written consent."

"Relax, Mike. They're not leaving the country. They're picking her up in the morning, and the three of them are spending the day at Familyland. Lucy thought it would be a nice, fun, kid-friendly place where she and Daniel could get to know Sophie better."

"Okay, but just to be on the safe side, make sure her passport stays here in the house."

"Aye, aye, detective."

"Diana!" It was Sophie calling from upstairs. "Goodnight. Thanks for pizza."

"Do you want me to come in?" Diana called back.

"Nope. I'm good. See you in the morning."

"Sweet dreams, sweetheart," Diana chirped.

"That's it?" I said. "She's been coming out to say goodnight for five months. Tonight she's phoning it in, and I'm not on the short list?"

"She's mad at you. She knows I'm willing to fight to keep her here, and you're not."

"I'm going to tuck her in," I said.

"I don't think she wants to be tucked."

"I don't care."

I went upstairs to Sophie's room. It was dark, except for the lotus flower night-light that slowly changed colors. I sat down on the edge of the bed as the soft glow of indigo transmuted to a soothing blue.

"I heard you're going to Familyland tomorrow," I said.

"Mmmm," she grunted, squinched up in a fetal position, her back to me.

"I know the head of security there."

"I know," she said. "You told me that when we went there this summer."

"You remember how he got us back-doored to all the good rides? I can call him, so you and Daniel and Lucy don't have to wait on any long lines."

"No thanks. The three of us will wait on line with all the other *families* at *Family*land."

Sophie Tan is a force to be reckoned with, and the way she skewered the word *family* twice in one sentence was testimony to her uncanny verbal skills. Even so, I had to remind myself that while she could go one-on-one with most adults intellectually, she still had the emotional development of an eight-year-old—one whose parents had left her to figure out life without them.

I'd have liked to tell her that I was in my forties and still working on the same process, but I didn't say a word. I just sat beside her for the next twenty minutes, listening to her soft breathing, and watching the lotus flower slowly morph through its rainbow of color.

CHAPTER 43

I SET THE silent alarm on my Fitbit for 5 a.m., threw on my running gear, and jogged three miles to a secluded spot on Santa Monica beach so I could watch the sun rise on the most important day of the year.

I've never really gotten the hang of meditating. My mind has trouble quieting down and reaching that elusive level of inner calm. But I gave it my best shot, taking long slow deep breaths, focusing on the sound of the waves, the smell of the salt air, and the cool sand beneath me.

Silently I repeated the single-word mantra Joanie had taught me when she decided to cram some peace and tranquility into my hectic cop life.

One.

"That's my secret word?" I asked her the day she unveiled it to me. "*One*? I thought you were going to give me some magical, mystical Sanskrit mantra that I could chant aloud to the deities."

"You mean like *Om Gum Ganapatayei Namah,*" she said.

"Yeah, that's got sex appeal. Can I use that?"

"You're not ready," she told me. "Just keep repeating the word 'one.' And no chanting. Just say it in your mind."

"One. You sure you don't mean *om*?" I said.

"Mike, you can't argue your way into a state of nirvana," she said. "Now in the words of the revered master Garab Dorje,

'Shut the fuck up and meditate.'"

And so, on that balmy Saturday morning, the eighteenth of October, I sat in silent reflection on a lonely strip of beach, as the sun broke orange and gold over the Pacific Ocean.

It was the second anniversary of Joanie's death, and while *two* seemed a much more appropriate mantra for the occasion, my somewhat enlightened spirit knew better, and I stuck with *one*.

I was pretty sure that Diana wouldn't know the significance of this date in my life. There were only two people who might hone in on it. Big Jim was one of them, but after our failed beer summit from the previous night I doubted that I'd be talking to him.

The other, of course, was Terry. Our plan for the morning was to have another long talk with Bruce Bower. In the twenty-four hours since he'd told us his story about being recruited to murder Wade Yancy, Terry and I had done a lot of solid police work, and we had a long list of new questions for him.

But first, breakfast. The Headlines Diner & Press Club on Kinross is one of our favorite places, and it's only a half mile from UCLA Med. Terry was already at a table when I got there. True to form, he went right for the heart of my day. Joanie.

"Two years," he said, as soon as I sat down. "It doesn't seem possible. How are you holding up?"

"I ran down to the beach to watch the sun rise," I said. "That helped. But I think I made a big mistake not telling Diana why I can't make a commitment to adopting Sophie. She's not happy with me, and the kid is downright pissed. She didn't say good night to me last night, and she wouldn't even look at me this morning."

"So come clean. Tell Diana what's going on."

"To what end? I'd rather wait till Tuesday, and I can tell her something beyond the speculation stage."

"Are the aunt and uncle willing to wait around till you make up your mind?"

"They have no choice. They can't get Sophie out of the country without my permission. However, they're doing their best to win her over. They're taking her to Familyland today."

"Familyland," Terry said. "It's been a year and a half since we saved that venerable institution from near extinction. Does Sophie know you walk on water in that theme park?"

"Everyone walks on water there, Biggs" I said. "They're cartoon characters. But it doesn't matter. I offered to pick up the phone and get Sophie the VIP treatment, but she turned me down."

"Damn, she is pissed at you."

Terry's cell rang. He looked at the caller ID and frowned. "Detective Biggs," he said.

He listened for thirty seconds, the frown on his face slowly turning into a scowl. "Thanks for the call, doc," he said. "You saved us a trip."

He hung up. "That was UCLA Med. Bruce Bower just died."

I shook my head and let the news sink in. We still had a lot of questions. We were going to have to get answers from someplace else.

"As long as we're not going to UCLA, I need to take some personal time," I said.

"Take all the time you need," Terry said. "I'll go to the office and catch up on some paperwork."

Terry didn't have to ask where I was going. He knew.

CHAPTER 44

I GOT IN the car, opened the glove compartment, and took out the CD mix that Joanie had made for me when we were first dating. She'd labeled it Show Tunes For Real Men. It was part of her long-range plan to broaden my limited cultural horizons.

I popped it in the player, pushed the random button, and turned up the volume. As if she'd planned it, the first song out of the box was "Oh, What A Beautiful Mornin'."

"Sure it is, Joanie. Sure it is," I said, as I headed west on Wilshire toward Woodlawn Cemetery.

"If you have to spend eternity in LA," Joanie had told me when she picked out her final resting place, "Woodlawn is your best option. It's got great views of the Pacific Ocean, the Santa Monica Mountains, and there's a Denny's a mile away that's open twenty-four hours."

The marker on her grave was simple. A bronze plaque set in granite at ground level, with her name, Joanellen Stockton Lomax, and the dates of her birth and death.

I bought some lilies from a flower vendor on Pico, set them down on the bed of green grass near her head, and took a knee.

"You're a real piece of work," I said to her. "Two years, and you're still surprising the shit out of me. I thought there were nine letters. *Nine*. And then out of the blue last night, Big Jim tells me there are 'a few more for special occasions.' He delivered the 'congratulations, Dad-to-be' letter last night.

"I read it two, or three, or thirty times. I just want you to know that I appreciate the sentiment, but I'm not sure I'm a Dad-to-be, and even if I am, it's not the way you might have pictured it, with my hand resting on my new wife's belly, and my face lighting up with every fetal kick. It's a long story—a lot has happened since I was here in July, but I'm guessing you have time."

I told her about Grandma Xiaoling's death, Carly's prison sentence, and the sudden opportunity to become the father of an eight-year-old girl I adored.

"So what's stopping me, you might ask. Good question. What do you know about white blood cell counts?"

I told her everything, bandying about the new medical terminology that was now burned into my brain—Chronic Myeloid Leukemia, Philadelphia chromosome, pathognomonic, bone marrow biopsy.

"Bottom line," I said, closing my eyes, "I don't want to say no to Sophie, but she's already lost a father and a mother, and if my doc comes back with bad news, I don't want her to have to go through the pain of losing me."

It doesn't matter if you're her father or not. She loves you. She'd be losing you either way, dummy.

I opened my eyes and scanned the cemetery. The nearest living soul was at least an acre away. My eyes welled up, and I felt the warm tears rolling down my cheeks.

I pounded the heel of my fist on the cool grass, and I let the dam burst wide open. I sobbed with an anguish known only to those who have lost a loved one in the prime of their life.

Dying is a part of living, Mike. Don't let Sophie get away because you want to spare her the pain of loss. If you knew I was going to die young, would you not have married me?

I smiled when I heard that. Joanie's logic never failed to ring true.

"God, I fucking miss you," I said, standing up.

I debated whether or not I should tell her about Dr. Kraus. She'd be upset about the murder, but then I'd have to get into the whole thing about Ovamax, and I wasn't ready to share that with her, especially if the worst of it were true.

My cell phone rang. "Sorry, it's Diana," I said, taking the call. "Hey, what's up?"

"Sophie's gone," Diana said. "She's missing."

I braced myself. "What do you mean 'missing'?"

"She was at Familyland with Daniel and Lucy. They don't know what happened. Once minute they had her, and the next minute she was gone."

"Call security. Ask for Brian Curry. It's Familyland for God's sake—she must have wandered off."

"Security is already involved. But Daniel and Lucy don't think she went off on her own. They're hysterical. They think she was taken."

"Meet me at Familyland," I said, and I raced to my car cursing the name of Jeremy Tan, and completely forgetting to say good-bye to my wife.

PART THREE

UP IN THE AIR

CHAPTER 45

AS SOON AS I peeled out of the cemetery my first instinct was to call Terry. I picked up the phone, then tossed it back on the front seat. There was nothing he could do except get crazy because there was nothing he could do. I was on my own.

Twenty minutes later Brian Curry called me. "We haven't found her yet," he said, "but we have a sighting. I'm on my way to Jackrabbit Junction to see if I can track her down."

"Can you call ahead to the ride operator and ask him to hold onto her?"

"Sorry, Mike," he said. "Every damn thing connected to this place goes by a cutesy name. Jackrabbit's not a ride. It's our major transportation hub. It's basically Grand Central Terminal for tens of thousands of guests and employees. We get five, six hundred buses rolling though there on a normal day—charters, airport and hotel shuttles, plus over thirty different metro and long-distance carriers, some of which come from as far as a hundred and fifty miles away."

"I'll meet you there," I said.

"Do you know where it is?"

"Not, but once I get in the park, somebody can—"

"Mike, it's not in the park. It's two miles from the main gate."

"*Two miles*? Then someone must have snatched her. An eight-year-old kid couldn't get that far on her own."

"This one could have. There are monorails running in and out of the park every six minutes. We picked Sophie up on the security feed. She got on a train about forty minutes ago and got off at Jackrabbit."

"Alone?"

"Hard to say. She was in the middle of a pack of people. I couldn't tell if she was with anyone, or if she used them as a beard to exit the property. I'm guessing she's smart enough to realize she'd get stopped by Security if we spotted her roaming around on her own."

"Smart doesn't begin to describe this kid," I said.

Ten minutes later I pulled into the sprawling transportation complex and headed straight for the cluster of police cruisers at the far end of the depot. Diana was already there, along with the comforting presence of the man whose job it was to protect the well-being of everyone who entered his utopian domain—Brian Curry.

I put my arm around Diana. "Brian thinks she got on a bus," she said.

"Emphasis on the word *think*," Brian said. "I can't tell for sure. The cameras are on a ninety-second sweep over here, so once she got off the monorail we couldn't stick with her. She could have bolted and taken off on foot. If she did get on a bus, we have no idea which one, or if she's alone."

"If she did hop a bus, what were her options at that hour of day?" I said.

"We've narrowed it down to six different LA county bus lines. Blue line, green, red, gold, white, and tan." He handed me a sheet of paper with a thumbnail route map for each one.

"Green is her favorite color," Diana said, looking at the maps. "And her last name is Tan."

"It's crazy to guess," Brian said. "I was just about to call the dispatchers and have them radio their drivers to pull over until we can get a unit out there to search each bus."

"Don't," I said. "If someone took her they're not going to wait around for the cavalry. They'll get off the bus as soon as it stops. If she's on her own, she'll do the same thing."

I studied the route maps. "Damn!" I said. "She's on the red line."

"How did you come up with that?" Brian said.

"Cop instinct," I said. "I'm going after her. How many backup units do you have here?"

"My people have no juice outside the park, so I put out a call to LAPD, county, and local. A dozen cars have showed up so far, and there are more on the way. Nothing rallies the troops like a missing kid."

"Here's the drill," I said. "Diana and I are going to chase down the red line, but just in case I'm wrong, send one unit out to stop and search each of the other five buses."

"I've got another half-dozen units available," Brian said. "You want me to send them home?"

"Hell no," I said, grabbing Diana by the hand and heading toward my car. "I'm just a private citizen who is about to break every traffic law in the books. I could use some lights and sirens to help me get where I'm going without getting arrested."

CHAPTER 46

"DO YOU THINK she's all right?" Diana asked as we barreled along the Pomona Freeway.

"I think she's more than all right," I said. "I think she's on that bus, laughing her ass off, and enjoying every minute of it."

"And you don't think Jeremy took her?"

"I did at first, but not now. He didn't know she'd be at Familyland, and even if he did, he'd have a car waiting in the parking lot."

"Why didn't you say that to Brian?"

"Because custody abductions get Amber Alerts and a slew of cop cars to run interference for us on the freeway. The kid flew the coop on her own—probably started scoping it out the minute she knew she was going to Familyland with Lucy and Daniel. I guarantee you she had a getaway plan and bus fare."

"And what makes you think she's on the red line?"

"Because when people are running away from a threat, they go where they can feel safe."

"We're safe," Diana said.

"*You* are, but I became a threat the minute I didn't agree to adopt her."

"Then where is she going?"

"To the one person she knows is not afraid to stand up to me."

Diana's eyes opened wide. "Big Jim," she said.

"The red line runs right through Riverside," I said. "She can walk to Big Jim's place from the bus stop."

"Oh, my God, do you think he knows she's coming?"

"No. Whatever other bad behavior Big Jim Lomax may be guilty of, he wouldn't let us spend a nanosecond worrying about a missing kid. However, once she gets to his house, he'll call us, tell us she's okay, and then grant her asylum, because he's convinced that I don't want her."

"He's not alone, Mike. Everyone is convinced that you don't want her."

"Of course I want her, damn it," I said, slamming my hand on the steering wheel.

"Then why—"

"Because she needs a father, and I don't know if I'm going to be around long enough to do the job!"

"What... what are you talking about?"

"I'm sorry," I said. "I've been holding out on you. I finally made up my mind to come clean. I was going to tell you tonight over a glass of wine, not on a freeway at a hundred and ten miles an hour."

"Mike, I don't care if we're on a rocket to the moon. Something's wrong. I've known it for days. Whatever it is, please... just tell me."

"That bullshit about Doug Heller calling me back to his office from a prostate exam—that was just a cover story. My white blood count was high, and when he took it a second time it went higher, so he sent me for a bone marrow biopsy. They're testing me for Chronic Myeloid Leukemia. I never heard of it, but I'm guessing you have."

Diana is a pediatric oncology nurse. "More often than I'd like to. Why didn't you tell me?"

"Why do you think? I won't have the results till Tuesday, and I didn't want you to worry."

"Mike, you're a cop. Are you remotely aware of the fact that I worry about you every day?"

"Yeah, I think you may have mentioned it two or three hundred times since we've been together."

"So in your infinite male wisdom you decided that it's okay if I worry about someone putting a bullet through your thick skull, but you want to spare me the possibility that you might have a treatable disease."

"When you put it like that, it sounds kind of stupid."

"It's beyond stupid," she said. "I thought you and I were in this relationship for the long haul."

"We are."

"Well, then bad stuff is going to happen. It's called life. I can handle that. What I can't handle is you sneaking around, keeping secrets, thinking you're going to spare me, when in fact what you're really doing is driving me insane trying to figure out what's wrong with you."

"Detective." It was my radio.

I keyed the mic. "Go ahead, officer."

"We've got the bus in sight."

"Pull him over and box him in, so that people looking out the windows know we mean business. But don't board. I'm getting on first."

"I'm going with you," Diana said. It wasn't police protocol, but at this point I was not about to argue with her.

CHAPTER 47

THE LEAD CRUISER rolled up alongside the bus and signaled the driver to pull over to the shoulder. He complied in a hurry, and a caravan of cars, their roof lights strobing red and blue surrounded him. A single CHP unit hung back a half mile to the rear to keep the traffic out of the right lane.

I put my badge around my neck, got out of the car, and walked toward the bus. Diana was right behind me. The driver opened the door, and we got on.

"LAPD, ladies and gentlemen," I said. "Please remain in your seats. This won't take long."

I let my eyes drift over the passengers. No Sophie.

I walked toward the back of the bus and slowly checked every row one by one. I was three-quarters of the way up the aisle when Diana's nails dug into my shoulder.

There was Sophie, slouched low in her seat, her head turned to the window, a baseball cap pulled down to her eyes.

She was sitting next to an attractive Asian woman in her early thirties. The kid knew she would attract less attention if it looked like she was travelling with an adult, and she had picked a perfect seatmate.

"Detective Mike Lomax, LAPD, ma'am," I said to the woman. "What's your name?"

"Suki Choi," she said.

"Ms. Choi, I'm looking for an eight-year-old girl. I think she's running off to New York to join the Rockettes."

The woman was a quick study. She stole a sideways glance at Sophie and winked at me. "I love the Rockettes," she said.

"Who doesn't?" I said, "but I'm afraid this kid is in for a big disappointment. She's only four feet tall, and to be a Rockette you've got to be at least five foot two."

"Five foot six," the lump in the baseball cap mumbled.

"She's also quite a talented young author," Diana said, "so it's possible she's not really running away. She could just be out there in search of something to write about."

"Did you happen to see her?" I asked. I shook my head vigorously, and Suki Choi played right along.

"No, detective," she said. "She sounds like a real keeper, but there's nobody here by that description. I hope you find her."

"Oh, I will," I said, leaning across the seat and talking directly into Sophie's ear. "Because Detective Mike Lomax always gets his man."

"Girl," the lump protested.

"Nice try, Sophie Tan," I said, "but I'm taking you downtown. You have the right to remain silent."

"Fat chance," she said, turning to face me. She held up her wrists. "Go ahead, copper, slap the bracelets on me."

Suki Choi laughed out loud.

"She's been spending a lot of time with cops," Diana said. "She's picked up the lingo."

"Come on, Sophie," I said, holding my arms out. "Are you ready to go home?"

"China's not my home."

"I'm not talking about China. I'm talking about going back to your home on Hill Street in Santa Monica, California."

"For how long?"

I shrugged. "I don't know. For as long as you can put up with me, Diana, Big Jim, Angel, Frankie, Izzy, and all the other people who love and adore you."

"Really?" Sophie said, tears welling up in her eyes.

"Really," Diana said.

"I'm not going to China?" Sophie said. Tears were streaming down her face, but she was grinning.

"Don't worry, kiddo," I said. "You're not going anywhere. You're staying right here with us."

Sophie bolted from her seat, jumped into my arms, and hugged me tight. I scooped Diana into the hug, and I stood there surrounded by a busload of dumbstruck passengers, strangely aware that despite what I'd been through over the past four days, I had never in my life felt so alive.

CHAPTER 48

"CAN WE GO to Big Jim's house and tell him the good news?" Sophie asked as soon as we were off the bus.

She could have asked for anything, and I'd have agreed. "Yes, but first we have some unfinished business to attend to," I said.

The three of us backtracked to Familyland where Aunt Lucy and Uncle Daniel were waiting in Brian's office. Sophie delivered a semi-sincere, but well-written apology and allowed herself to be hugged, scolded, and hugged some more until the Zhangs finished letting off their hours of pent-up emotional steam.

As soon as her penance was done, Sophie launched, unscripted, into "*You can go back to China now because I'm staying here with Mike and Diana, thank you very much.*"

Daniel and Lucy looked at me, and I nodded. "There's a lot of logistics we have to talk about, but that's the plan as of now," I said. "How do you folks feel about it?"

"You're asking us?" Lucy said, laughing. "We only had her for a few hours, and we lost her."

"You didn't lose her," Diana said. "You were outsmarted. There's a difference."

"Even so," Daniel said, "we are much too old to go through this on a daily basis. We'd be happy for Sophie to stay here with you, but we still have one obstacle to contend with."

"Let's talk about it over dinner," I said. "I called Angel, and she and Big Jim are expecting us."

I took Brian Curry aside and thanked him for pulling out all the stops.

He shrugged off the thank-you and rubbed a hand over his smooth-shaved bronze pate. "Hey man, whatever it takes to help you get your little girl back."

My little girl. The words both warmed me to the core and weighed heavily on my mind as we drove to my father's place in Riverside.

Frankie and Izzy were there already there, and Sophie burst out of the car to let my brother know that he was about to become her uncle.

"And what will I be?" Izzy asked.

"Duh," Sophie said. "My uncle's girlfriend."

"Where are Big Jim and Angel?" Sophie said.

"Angel's waiting for you in the kitchen," Frankie said. "Big Jim will be there in a minute."

Sophie raced to the kitchen door, and Frankie frowned at me. "Don't shoot the messenger, bro, but Dad's waiting for you in the truck barn. Brace yourself for one of his legendary father-son talks."

"Gosh, I can't wait. I haven't had one of those since ..." I looked at my watch. "Oh, I think it was about eight o'clock last night."

Big Jim has a small office in the truck barn with a desk, a file cabinet, a fridge, and two chairs.

"Congratulations on coming to your senses," he said, giving me a hug and a cold can of beer. "You're going to make a great father."

"I'm not so sure," I said. "I haven't gotten the annoying meddling part down yet, but I think I can learn."

"Speaking of which," he said, "what can I do to help you convince Jeremy that you're a better father for Sophie than he is?"

"I thought about that a lot on the drive over here," I said. "You can help, but I hate to ask."

"Are you kidding me? Just say the word, and I'm all over it."

"You're sure you don't mind?"

"Jesus, Mike, I'm your father. Of course I don't mind."

"Okay. I need you to write it all down," I said, sitting down and popping the top on my beer.

He grabbed a pad and pencil. "Go ahead," he said.

"Stay out of it," I said. "Thanks for the beer."

I got up, walked out, and left him sitting in the truck barn, fuming.

CHAPTER 49

"SO HOW DID Sophie like Familyland?" Terry asked when I got to the squad room on the next morning.

"Funny thing about that," I said. "You want the long version or the short version?"

"At this hour? The shorter the better."

"She ran away from the aunt and uncle, hopped on a bus, Brian called in a dozen units to help me track her down, I did, I promised her she could stay here with us forever, and then I told Diana that I might have leukemia."

"Okay, you've piqued my interest," Terry said. "I think I'll go for the longer version."

I gave it to him.

"Why the hell didn't you call me as soon as you found out the kid ran away?"

"You sound like my father," I said. "The truth is, I thought about calling you, but I didn't know what to ask you to do."

"That's the problem with you, Lomax. You have no leadership skills."

"But he'll still make sergeant before you, dickwad," a voice said.

We looked up. Kilcullen had come through the door and was headed straight at us, looking even crankier than usual.

"Brendan," Terry said, "what an unexpected pleasure to gaze

upon your smiling Irish countenance on this glorious Sunday morning. What can we do for you?"

"You can kiss my Irish ass, Biggs."

"Ass kissing is not my strong suit, sir."

"Shut up! You know why I'm here. I've been duly notified that you plan to be asking the CEO of Chilton-Winslow a bunch of stupid-ass questions."

"Are you serious, lieutenant?" I said. "Did Mel Berger actually send you to hold our hands in the middle of a homicide investigation?"

"Do you think it was *my* idea to spend my day off telling you how to do your job? Berger asked you guys not to harass Egan Granville. All you had to do was say yes, then go off and do whatever you want, but Biggs basically responded with a one-finger salute. Berger turned around and put it on me."

"So are you here to tell us not to interview Granville?" I said

"Hell, no. I figure you've got a good reason, but rather than try to explain that shit to a politician, I told him I'd go with you and keep you from embarrassing the department and the mayor. Now, why don't you bring me up to speed."

We took Kilcullen through everything we'd learned about Ovamax, including the fact that Amanda Dunbar told us that Granville was responsible for keeping the drug on the market for two years after he knew it was killing patients.

"She's got to be lying," Kilcullen said. "The President of the United States nominated Granville for a cabinet post. He was vetted by Congress."

"And now he's going to be vetted by LAPD," I said. "Even if he's not guilty of anything, he's probably high on our killer's hit list."

Terry opened up the annual report we'd found in Charlie Brock's apartment. "Dead, dead, and dead," he said, pointing to Carolyn Butler, Kristian Kraus, and Wade Yancy. "Dunbar is an obvious target, but we paid her a visit, and from the looks of it, she's hunkered down and ready for Armageddon."

"If what she said is even remotely true, then Granville's ass is also in the crosshairs," Kilcullen said. "Are you planning to tell him that his life is in danger?"

"We'd rather arrest him for criminally negligent manslaughter," Terry said, "but that's not in the cards. We're ready to move out. Are you sure you want to ride with us?"

"It's the last thing I want to be doing, but the deputy mayor wants someone with political savvy to finesse the meeting with Granville," Kilcullen said.

"In that case, you definitely should tag along," Terry said. "Like I said, ass kissing isn't my strong suit."

CHAPTER 50

WE ARRIVED AT Chilton-Winslow in Culver City at 9:30. Marion McGirr, Granville's executive guard dog, kept us waiting at the security desk for twenty minutes and was less than thrilled when she saw that we'd added yet another cop to the mix.

"Really?" she grumbled as soon as Kilcullen introduced himself. "Now there are *three* of you? This is getting to be like the Spanish Inquisition."

"Sorry if we blindsided you, Ms. McGirr," Kilcullen said, his Irish charm on point, "but the mayor's office felt that a man of Mr. Granville's stature warranted a personal visit from the unit commander."

"That explains why *you're* here, lieutenant," McGirr said. "Why you still need these other two escapes me, but we don't have time to debate. Mr. Granville should be arriving in ten minutes. Let's go up to the helipad."

We took the elevator to the roof, where three men in red coveralls were waiting for the helicopter to land.

"According to everything I read," Kilcullen said, making small talk, "the Senate is likely to confirm Mr. Granville's appointment tomorrow."

"It's more than *likely*," McGirr said. "The vote takes place at 10 a.m. Washington time, and we've already scheduled a board meeting for noon our time, so Mr. Granville can step down from Chilton-Winslow. And then, as he will say in his farewell remarks, he'll be moving 'from the medicine cabinet to the President's cabinet.'"

"They're coming in," one of the red coveralls called out.

"Who else is travelling with Mr. Granville?" Kilcullen said.

McGirr looked at him sharply. "Why would you ask?"

Kilcullen is a smart cop. He'd studied the pictures in the annual report, and he knew that Granville might not be the only target on board. But that was none of Marion McGirr's damn business.

He smiled. "Senior executives have a broader perspective than everyone else, Ms. McGirr. I'm sure you'd agree that it would be an injustice for us to be surrounded by people of that caliber and not ask them a few questions that might lead to our understanding of why Dr. Kraus was killed."

That pacified her, and she glanced at the manifest. "In addition to Mr. Granville, we have Nolan Sutter, our Chief Financial Officer, Ernst Zweig, Executive VP Manufacturing, and Arvin Boynton-Forbes, our Global Ethics and Compliance Officer."

Terry put his hand over his mouth to cover the smirk that blossomed when she said Global Ethics.

I looked at Kilcullen. He nodded. He'd recognized the names. We had just seen their faces in the annual report.

The chopper was about half a mile out, and we watched it approach. About two hundred feet shy of the building, it slowed and hovered.

The landing team looked up, then at each other. The crew chief picked up his radio. "CW Air, this is CW Ground. Is there a problem?"

No answer.

He keyed the mic again. "CW Air, this is CW Ground. You're clear to land. Do you read me?"

Still no answer.

McGirr snatched the radio out of his hand. "Captain Elliott, this is Marion McGirr. What the hell is going on up there?"

"Ms. McGirr," a voice responded. "I've heard so much about you from Captain Elliott."

"Who is this," she demanded, "and where is my pilot?"

"The captain is back at the terminal, no doubt silently cursing out the makers of Duck Tape for producing such a strong, durable product," the voice came back. "My name is Charlie. Your pilot this morning is Dahlia. We won't be landing today. We will, however, be dropping off several of your board members. The first to disembark will be your Corrupt Financial Officer."

A few seconds passed, and two men appeared in the open doorway of the aircraft. I recognized Charlie Brock immediately. I didn't know the man standing in front of him, but I was sure McGirr would.

"Oh, my God," she said. "It's Nolan Sutter."

Sutter clawed at the door frame, desperately trying to fight his way back into the chopper. But the corporate number cruncher was no match for the veteran combat Marine.

For one brief moment Sutter was the focal point of a tableau, frozen in the sky fifteen hundred feet over the West Coast Campus of Chilton-Winslow. The next moment his body was hurtling toward the ground, legs kicking, arms flailing, the screams that came from his open mouth never to be heard, drowned out by the rhythmic drone of the rotors.

But nothing could mask the sickening sound of shattering bone and ripping flesh as the CFO of one of the most powerful pharmaceutical companies on the planet exploded onto the concrete.

Marion McGirr covered her eyes just before the moment of impact, and while there was nothing in our police training that said we couldn't have done the same, Terry, Kilcullen, and I all watched in collective horror until the deadly free fall came to its inevitable violent conclusion.

Marion screamed, and Kilcullen, shock still etched on his face, instinctively sprang to her side to shield her from the mangled mass of blood and viscera on the ground below.

Charlie's voice came back over the radio. "I would like to extend a special welcome to our guests from LAPD, Detectives Lomax and Biggs. Gentlemen, I can't tell you what a wonderful surprise it is to see that you're here just in time to watch our little show. That was Act One. Now why don't you hop on La Cienega and meet us at 5801 Wilshire Boulevard for Act Two."

CHAPTER 51

I'VE WITNESSED VIOLENT deaths before, a few even more mind-searing than the cold-blooded murder of Nolan Sutter. I'm trained to dissociate from the horror, control my gut-level human reaction, and respond to the emergency.

Marion McGirr had no such training. She broke loose from Kilcullen, raised a fist to the sky, and began screaming into the radio.

The noise of the blades whirring overhead made most of it unintelligible, but I managed to pick out "wife and three children."

Kilcullen grabbed the radio and tried to calm her down, but the woman was in shock, and she began pounding on his chest and wailing at him to do something.

Terry and I helped get her under control, and we ordered the landing crew chief to stay with her till the paramedics arrived. Then the three of us raced for the elevator.

As soon as we started to descend Kilcullen began barking into the ground-to-air radio. "This is Lieutenant Brendan Kilcullen, LAPD. There is nowhere you can go in a helicopter that you won't be caught. Land now and give yourselves up."

Land now? Charlie Brock was a trained assassin who had commandeered a helicopter, kidnapped the soon-to-be Secretary of Health and Human Services, and publicly murdered a high-ranking executive of a major corporation. *He wasn't about to land*. Kilcullen's request was as fruitless as McGirr's tirade. I'm sure he knew it, but he was following police protocol.

"I repeat," he said, "land now. You will be caught, and you will only make the consequences worse for yourselves if you kill any more innocent people."

"News flash, lieutenant," Charlie's voice came back. "There are no innocent people on this aircraft. Myself included."

The elevator reached the lobby, and we ran toward the parking lot. The chopper was still hovering overhead. As soon as we were in the car, the pilot banked to the left, climbed, and headed for their next drop-off point.

Kilcullen was already on his cell phone to Dispatch. "I'm at Chilton-Winslow Pharmaceuticals on Bristol Parkway, Culver City, where a helicopter dropped a man from fifteen hundred feet."

I couldn't hear the other side of the conversation, but his face turned red, and he exploded into the phone. "Of course, there's a fucking fatality! Send the coroner and tell him to bring a fucking spatula and a sponge. I also need a bus on the scene to treat people for trauma."

He took a beat to gain his composure. "Detectives Lomax and Biggs and I are on the ground in pursuit of a royal blue Bell helicopter, which is reportedly heading for five-eight-zero-one Wilshire. I want a bird in the air tracking them, and I need all available cars to report to that location, Code 3. Round up as many CHP units as you can to clear traffic along La Cienega, Slauson, and whatever else is between Bristol and 5801 Wilshire. Have them cordon off the area for six blocks in every direction and move all civilians off the streets. And the goddamn press is going to be all over this, so for God's sake, keep them at a distance. Odds are these crazy bastards are going to splatter another body on the pavement."

"I don't think you have to worry about that, Lieutenant," I said.

"What the hell are you talking about?" he boomed. "You heard what that psycho said. *Act Two*. Are you telling me you don't think he's going to toss another body?"

"Oh, he's going to toss one," I said. "But not to the pavement."

"What are you talking about?"

"I just checked the location on the GPS. There's not a lot of pavement at 5801 Wilshire."

"Then what the hell is there?"

"Tar. Acres and acres of tar."

CHAPTER 52

"IT'S KIND OF inspired don't you think?" Terry said as we sped along Hauser Boulevard, keeping pace with the chopper.

"What's inspired?" Kilcullen said.

"The La Brea Tar Pits," Terry said. "I mean, if you're going to drop these evil drug lords out of a chopper, then the tar pits is the perfect place to do it."

"Do I have to remind you that your job is to prevent that from happening?" Kilcullen said.

"And do I have to remind you that on Day One my partner told you that Kraus had been his wife's fertility doctor, and you said, 'no connection, no conflict'? So now that it turns out Kraus was knowingly, willfully injecting her with a drug that killed her, it's hard for me hang onto that 'no conflict' shit."

"You wear the shield, you do the job," Kilcullen said.

"Hey, I'm not saying I won't protect and serve. I'm just saying it would be righteously poetic if they drop one of those fuckers in a lake of bubbling oil. And for the record, if I fail to stop them, I guarantee you I won't lose any sleep over it."

Kilcullen had the good sense not to pursue the discussion.

As soon as we turned onto Wilshire it was clear that Kilcullen's order to cordon off the area was wishful thinking at best. It was a beautiful Sunday in October, and the Pits, one of the city's biggest attractions, was bubbling over with tourists as well as tar.

There was no time for an evacuation. Whatever went down was going to be a public spectacle.

We got out of the car and watched as the helicopter took position fifteen hundred feet over the largest pool of liquid petroleum—the lake pit with its life-size fiberglass statues of mammoths. Charlie appeared in the doorway along with two more potential victims. I recognized them from the annual report—Zweig, the manufacturing boss, and Boynton-Forbes, the world's most unethical ethics officer.

"Detective Lomax." It was Charlie. "Pick one."

Kilcullen handed me the radio. "Charlie," I said. "Don't do it."

"You're telling me not to kill at least one of them?" he said. "You of all people, Lomax? These bastards killed your wife."

I looked at Terry. "How the hell does he know that? I never told him about Joanie."

Terry shook his head.

"Charlie, I know what they did," I said. "But I'm a cop. Turn them over and let a jury decide."

"I'm not going to live long enough to see a jury trial," Charlie said. "I gave you the option. Pick one."

"I can't do that."

"Fair enough," he said.

He pushed. Hard. Twice. And the two men came tumbling out of the aircraft.

The crowd, which had become uncontainable, let out a collective scream as the two corporate officers plummeted from the sky, and ten seconds later were claimed by the same black ooze that had swallowed mastodons and saber-toothed cats eons before them.

"Mother of God," Kilcullen said.

As far as I knew, Granville was still alive. I radioed up to Charlie. "You made your point. Stop now. Please."

"I can't stop," Charlie said. "I get paid piecework, and I've still got one more piece to dispose of."

Kilcullen grabbed the radio from me. "This is Lieutenant Brendan Kilcullen. Egan Granville has been nominated by the President of the United States to be Secretary of Health and Human Services. You toss him out of that chopper, and LAPD won't be the only ones dogging your ass."

"I'm not tossing him just yet, but as taxpaying citizens we've got some serious questions to put to Mr. Granville about his policies and procedures at Chilton-Winslow."

"Cut the shit, you son of a bitch," Kilcullen bellowed.

"You sound angry, chief. You should be thanking me. I saved the county a fortune in legal expenses it would cost them to prosecute the two murderers I just delivered. All that's left for you to do is fish them out of the muck. Have fun."

Charlie stepped back inside the chopper as it lifted up and flew off.

This time he didn't tell us where he was headed. And he didn't wait for us to follow.

CHAPTER 53

TERRY AND I spend so much time moaning about what a pain in the ass Kilcullen is that we tend to forget that he didn't pick up a gold bar because of his irrepressible charm.

Kilcullen is a kickass cop. As soon as the bodies hit the cauldron of bubbling black soup, he yelled at me and Terry to track the chopper. Then he grabbed a bullhorn, and the very same abrasive asshole who had impounded our candy machine took charge of organizing the troops, dispersing the crowd, and opening the roads for emergency vehicles.

In ten minutes he turned the crime scene from bedlam to controlled chaos and finally to a reasonable semblance of order. Then he passed the baton to a cohort from the Wilshire station and rejoined us. "Do we have a bird in the air?" he asked.

"Air Five is on his tail," Terry said. "The jacked chopper headed due west. He was over Roxbury Park thirty seconds ago."

The radio came alive. "Air Five to Six Henry One."

"Go ahead, Air Five," Terry called back.

"The Bell is at six hundred feet and dropping. I think they're putting her down."

"Where?"

"They're on Constellation crossing Avenue of the Stars, and hold on, detective... son of a ... they're hovering over the Westfield Century City mall."

We all knew what was coming next.

"Six Henry One, your bird is down. He landed on the roof of the mall and killed the engine."

"Mike," Terry said, "scramble some units to Century City."

The radio chirped again. "Six Henry One, your perps are on the run. White female in a dark flight suit, and two white males, one in a camo jacket, the other in a blue business suit."

"The suit is not a perp. Repeat, he is not a perp," Terry said. "He's a hostage."

"Camo jacket just hustled him to an exit door. The three of them are gone—disappeared into the mall."

I had Dispatch on my radio. "I need units at Century City—as many as you can roll. Code 3."

"Most of my cars are at the tar pits," the dispatcher said. "I can pull them in from Rampart and Southwest."

"That won't cut it," Kilcullen yelled at me. "They wouldn't have landed there unless they had a car waiting. They'll be in the wind before we have units in position. Tell her to contact Westside Security and shut the mall down."

"Boss, we can seal off all vehicle exits," I said, "but they can walk out of any one of a hundred different doors on foot. They're too smart to leave a car in the garage. It's probably waiting for them outside."

Terry grabbed at the last straw. He radioed Air Five. "You saw what they were wearing—camo jacket, blue suit. If they're still on foot you might be able to spot them from the air and see what vehicle they get into."

"Detective, do you know how many ways there are to get in out of that place?" the pilot said. "Plus there's construction scaffolding covering the entire northeast corner, which is probably why they picked this mall instead of any one of a dozen others. It's a long shot at best."

"Right now it's the only shot we've got."

We stayed on the air with our spotter, but after ten minutes it was over. "No trace," Air Five called in, "and we just got a call. Drive-by in Inglewood. We've got shooters to chase down. We're out."

"Thanks," Terry said. He turned to Kilcullen. "We lost them."

"Shit," he said. "So you're telling me that these lunatics kidnapped a member of the President's cabinet on *my* watch."

"If it's any consolation," Terry said, "he wasn't confirmed yet."

"Not confirmed is a fucking asterisk," Kilcullen said. "The picture in the paper tomorrow morning will be me standing there yelling into a bullhorn while the goddamn Secretary of whatever dumbass department he's in charge of disappears right from under my nose."

My cell phone rang. A blocked number. I took the call and put it on speaker.

"Detective Lomax," the voice on the other end said. "Crazy weather we're having. Partly cloudy and raining corporate executives."

It was Charlie Brock. Kilcullen recognized the voice and screamed at the phone. "Did you hear what I said before, asshole? You may have a beef with some drug company, but you are fucking with the Washington power establishment. Let Granville go now."

"Hey, is that you again, chief?" Charlie said. "Lomax, tell your boss not to fret. We'll turn Granville loose."

"When?" I said.

"After the trial."

"What trial?"

"That's why I called you," Charlie said. "It's the day of reckoning for the Chilton-Winslow evil empire. We're going to live stream it on the web, and I want to make sure you tune in to the Egan Granville-Amanda Dunbar Show."

"You're putting Dr. Dunbar on trial too?" I said.

Charlie laughed. "I guess you haven't figured it out yet, have you, detective? Amanda Dunbar isn't on trial. She's the injured party. She's the plaintiff, the judge, and the jury."

The pieces of the puzzle all fell in at once, and I wanted to kick myself for not seeing it. Dunbar was one of the only people who knew that Joanie was one of the Ovamax victims. That's how Charlie found out. Dunbar told him.

"I work for Amanda," Charlie said. "Best damn boss I ever had. She pays half a million a pop for every one of those white-collar murderers we eliminate. And you know what's the best part?"

I didn't say a word. I knew he'd answer his own question.

"It all came from the blood money Chilton-Winslow paid her to take the fall for their crimes."

CHAPTER 54

RUPERT SIMMS HADN'T broken the law in thirty-seven years, but when Charlie Brock offered him a hundred thousand dollars for one simple job, he jumped at it. "I can't say no at this stage of my life," he'd said, adding with a laugh, "That'd be Stage IV, in case you was wonderin'."

He sat behind the wheel of the van and tapped the numbers into the calculator on his iPhone for the third time. No mistake about it. He would have had to drive a UPS truck for six thousand two hundred and fifty hours to make what Charlie was paying him to drive about ten miles.

He knew it wasn't Charlie's money. Charlie and Dahlia were just worker bees like him. But he didn't want to know nothing more about nothing. All he cared about was that a hundred large was a sweet chunk of change to leave behind for his sisters and their kids.

He heard the chopper approaching, and he looked up. Sure enough, just like Charlie said, the LAPD air force was right behind him.

They'd done a dry run the day before, and once Charlie and Dahlia were out of the helicopter it would take them two and a half minutes to get from the roof to the exit where the construction was outside The Container Store.

He started the van, waited for the signal, then pulled out of his parking spot on Pandora Avenue. Two and a half minutes later he rolled slowly past the construction on Century Park West, stopping just long enough to board his three passengers.

"Clothes off," Charlie said to Granville as Rupert turned onto Overland Avenue.

Granville removed his suit jacket and tie. He'd offered them a million dollars when they hijacked his helicopter. Then five when they killed Sutter, and twenty million when Boynton-Forbes and Zweig were hurled into the tar pits. They hadn't even blinked. He wondered if the old black guy driving the van could be swayed.

"Shirt and pants," Charlie ordered. "Leave the underwear. If you shit yourself, that's your problem."

"I'll pay you sixty million dollars to let me go," Granville said, stepping out of his pants. "Split it three ways, that's twenty million apiece."

"Dahlia and I aren't interested," Charlie yelled at the driver. "How about you, Rupert?"

"Hell no," Rupert hollered, making the right turn onto Olympic Boulevard. "That's the kind of money can fuck a body up. I'm fine the way I is, but I wouldn't mind getting my hands on that fancy blue suit he's shucking. The man's about my size. I mean if you think he's done with it."

"It's all yours," Charlie said, tossing an orange jumpsuit at Granville. "Dress for success, Egan. You gonna be a felon, you gotta look like a felon."

Granville put on the jumpsuit, then Dahlia sat him on the floor and covered his mouth with duct tape.

Charlie called Amanda. "Hey, Doc, everything went smooth."

"I know," she said. "I've been watching the Twitter feed. There were a couple of tweets when you tossed out Sutter, but once you got to the tar pits people started posting pix and OMGs and WTFs like mad. Now you're trending. #LAChopperDropper."

Charlie laughed out loud and repeated the hashtag for Dahlia and Rupert.

"These people have no idea what's coming next," Charlie said. "You ready?"

"I'm just waiting for the star of the show," Amanda said.

"We're almost there."

"Then it's time for you to call Detective Lomax."

"I still think that's a bad idea, Amanda."

"Listen to me, Charlie. We might not have gotten every last one of them, but we got the ringleaders, and the big fish is on his way in. As soon as we're done with him I want you, Dahlia, and Rupert to get your mercenary asses as far away from LA as possible. We've had a great run. Thanks. I'll see you all in heaven."

Charlie laughed. "*Heaven*? You sure about that?"

"Charlie, after I get through with Egan Granville, God Himself is going to personally open the gates and thank us for fixing his fuckup. Now make that call."

He hung up and looked across the van at his beautiful Israeli lover. Dahlia nodded her head. "Do it."

Charlie dialed the phone. "Detective Lomax," he said as soon as the cop picked up. "Crazy weather we're having. Partly cloudy and raining corporate executives."

CHAPTER 55

MAJOR CRIME SCENES take on a personality of their own, and the best way to describe this one was *three-ring circus*. Everyone wanted a front-row seat. And not just the media hounds and paparazzi. Within minutes after the shit hit the tar, the roads were jammed with amateur gawkers, gapers, and ghouls of every stripe.

"Screw Familyland," Terry said, a wide grin lighting up his muley mug. "This is the hottest tourist attraction in town."

Just as I finished the phone call with Charlie Brock a gleaming black fifty-foot Incident Command Post docked on South Curson Avenue, and the door opened.

"Dudes." It was Muller. He was wearing baggy shorts and the ugliest Hawaiian shirt I'd ever seen.

"Hate the shirt. Dig the ride," Terry said. "Where'd you get it?"

"Emergency Ops. She was going to roll with or without me," he said. "I just happened to be close enough and fast enough to jump on. Welcome aboard."

"Jesus," Terry said, as soon as we got inside. "It's like the Millennium Falcon in here."

"Rrrrr-gggrrhhhg," Muller responded in perfect Wookie.

"Mike and I need to get on the Internet," Terry said. "You got Wi-Fi on this contraption?"

"It's got about two million bucks' worth of high-tech bells and whistles. Why don't you tell me what's going on in case you need someone who knows what buttons to push."

We brought him up to speed, then the three of us sat down in front of a wall of monitors. Muller scanned the Internet looking for the live stream Charlie had promised, while Terry and I surfed the broadcast channels, which featured talking heads posing preposterous theories about a crime scene they knew absolutely nothing about.

Ten minutes into it, Kilcullen stormed through the door. "*Homeland Security*?" he boomed. "I understand the PC, the mayor, and the governor, but why the hell is Homeland fucking Security crawling up my butt?"

"Probably because one of these news assholes told his co-asshole that this had all the overtones of a terrorist attack," Terry said.

"Why the hell would he say that?"

"They're paid to talk, boss," Terry said. "Making sense is optional. One reporter said she heard it was a Hollywood movie stunt gone wrong, so don't be surprised if you also get a call from the Academy."

"Got it!" Muller said.

"Got what?" Kilcullen asked.

"The live stream link just hit the Twitter feed."

"I have no idea what the hell you just said."

"I'll translate," Terry said. He put an arm around Kilcullen. "Muller just found out what channel your show is going to be on, grandpa. You want some nice hot cocoa while we watch?"

"Bite me," Kilcullen said, shaking Terry loose. "Turn the damn thing on."

Muller hit the link and a title card came on:

THE TRIAL OF EGAN GRANVILLE

Below that was a brief background on the man, the crimes he was accused of, and an invitation to the public to weigh in on the proceedings. In the bottom right-hand corner was a countdown clock. The trial was still thirty minutes away.

"If she's got Granville," Kilcullen said, "what the hell is she waiting for?"

"An audience," I said. "She's giving it time to go viral."

"She's also giving us time," Terry said. "We've got a half hour. More than we need to check in with CSU."

Kilcullen stayed in the truck, and Terry and I walked to the lake pit where Jessica Keating was kneeling beside two tar-covered bodies.

"How the hell did you pull those two out of the muck so fast?" Terry said. "I thought you'd be dredging this hole forever."

"It's not really a hole," she said. "The tar, even in places where it's bubbling, is maybe only about six inches deep."

"Son of a bitch," Terry said. "So what you're saying is they should've called it the La Brea Tar Puddles."

She laughed. "Doesn't matter what you call it. They're both very dead. Which is what happens when you drop people from a quarter of a mile straight up. This guy lost a leg on impact, and the other one's head blew apart."

"We're going to try to catch the guys who dropped them. We'll be in the truck if you need us."

"It's going to be a while," she said. "My team is still trying to fish brains and body parts out of the soup. I won't be able to get you positive IDs until I get them back to the lab and clean them up. Plus I understand you left me a third guy over in Culver City."

"Yeah," Terry said, "but like they say in the cigarette ads, that one's got a lot less tar."

Jessica is one of Terry's best audiences, and I could hear her laughing as we walked back to the command post for the countdown.

CHAPTER 56

THE CLOCK ON the screen hit zero, and a picture faded up. A narrow table, Egan Granville in an orange jumpsuit seated at one end, Amanda Dunbar on the opposite side, a 9mm Glock in front of her. She had on a white lab coat, her copper-red wig gone, the full effects of her chemo on display.

As the picture burned into my brain, the irony and the hopeless reality of my situation hit me hard. My job was to save the man responsible for my wife's death and arrest the crusader whose dying mission was to bring him to justice.

There were no introductions. The viewing audience had more than enough time to get the backstories on the two adversaries.

"The senate confirmation hearings are over, Egan," Dunbar said in a strong, clear voice. "This time you're on trial for murder."

"Trial?" Granville spat out. "Why don't you call it what it is? A kangaroo court presided over by a cold-blooded killer who just paid to have three innocent men put to death."

"I'm not the only cold-blooded killer in the room," Dunbar said. "And they were far from innocent. Neither were the three others I paid to have killed."

"So if you're judge, jury, and executioner, why bother with this charade? Why don't you shoot me now and get it over with?"

"Because that would make you look like a victim, Egan, and

that is one title I refuse to let you share with the women you let die or the families you let suffer because of your greed."

"*My* greed? You created Ovamax, doctor. You made millions of dollars, and when your formulation was finally proven to be lethal I was the one who pulled the product off the market, while you walked away scot-free with millions more."

"That's the same story you told the Senate. Do you think they believed you?"

"We'll know when they vote on my nomination tomorrow morning, won't we, Dr. Dunbar?"

"How about the American people? Do you think they'll believe you?"

Granville sneered. "With all due respect to the American people, they don't get a vote."

"Actually, they do. We're streaming these proceedings live to millions, and that's the beauty of the Internet. There's no shortage of opinions, is there?"

"There's no shortage of technological talent either. I'll pay a million dollars to the first hacker who pinpoints your signal, calls the authorities and gets me out of here."

"That's your solution to everything, isn't it? Buy your way out. Like when you ramrodded that Alzheimer drug through clinical trials and wound up with twenty-seven documented cases of irreversible brain damage. How much did it cost you to sweep that one under the rug? Fifty million? Sixty? What's a human life worth these days, Egan?"

Granville sprang from his seat, and she grabbed the gun. He sat back down. "Did you ever run a company?" he bellowed.

She didn't answer. She held the gun in one hand and a remote control in the other. She used it to slowly let the camera move in on Granville.

"Do you even have any idea what it's like to run a major biotech enterprise like Chilton-Winslow? Do you know how many people depend on us? And I'm not just talking about the sixty-three thousand employees who count on us to pay for the roofs over their heads, or the food on their tables, or their kids' educations. I'm talking about the hundreds of millions of people in every corner of the planet waiting for us to come up with the next wonder drug that can make them whole again, keep them from dying, even put babies in their bellies when the good Lord Himself couldn't do it. They all want miracles. Straw into gold. Water into wine. Day in, day out," he said, his eyes seething with unrestrained disgust. "How many people do you think could run a company like that, Dr. Dunbar? Could you?"

The camera was tight on his face. His teeth were clenched, and his upper lip quivered.

"I didn't think so," he spit out, when it was clear that his question would go unanswered.

The camera pulled back out of the close up and returned to the wide shot.

"You're right," Amanda said softly. "A lot of people look to you to make the impossible seem possible. Doctors, patients, hospitals, governments... Chilton-Winslow research has helped lower the infant mortality rate across the entire continent of Africa by twelve percent over the past decade."

Granville's body relaxed.

"There's only one major constituency we haven't talked about," Dunbar said. "Investors. Nobody is rooting for you harder than the people who are going to make money if you're successful."

"It's a business," Granville said, the anger returning quickly.

"Oh, I get it," she said. "You're in the business of making miracles. Like God."

"I never said I was God!"

"And you're not! Because God doesn't have stockholders looking over His shoulder. God doesn't have a board of directors or bottom-line responsibilities. But you do, don't you, Egan?"

"Damn right I do. I repeat—it's a business!"

"So if you're trying to cure Alzheimer's, or put babies in bellies, you've got to expect some setbacks along the way. A little brain damage here, a few cases of ovarian cancer there—it's all part of the cost of doing business. And you're right. I couldn't do that job, Egan. Because when people start dying on my watch, my instinct as a scientist is to pull back, to cut my losses. That's why I asked you to go back to the safer version of Ovamax when the new one turned out to be so deadly. And you agreed, didn't you?"

"It shut you up."

"And how long was the old formulation back in circulation before you realized that it wasn't going to produce as many miracles, or make as much money?"

"Go to hell."

"I guess that means you knew all along. You just ran the old shit through the pipeline long enough for me to believe you, and then you went back to business as usual until the FDA picked up on the mounting death toll two years later."

"Fuck the FDA. Did they pick up on the fact that tens of thousands of women who desperately wanted children had their dream come true? The world is filled with happy, healthy, bouncing babies because of the decision I made. It's a tragedy that some women took the risk and died, but it was their risk to take."

"Be sure to repeat that to the LAPD homicide detective who comes here to pick you up," Amanda said. "Ask him if he and his wife would have taken the same risk if they had all the facts that you had."

"What LAPD homicide detective is she talking about?" Kilcullen said.

My cell phone vibrated. It was a text from Charlie Brock.

33°58'52.5"N 118°27'27.9"W

I held the coordinates up for Kilcullen to see.

He nodded. "I guess that answers my question."

CHAPTER 57

"HERE'S THE DEAL," I said to Kilcullen as Muller zeroed in on the coordinates. "You are not putting their twenty out over the air so that every asshole with a scanner can race to see who gets there first to claim Granville's million-dollar prize. Nobody gets the money, and nobody but me gets the collar. Any questions?"

"Just one," Kilcullen said. "Which one of them are you arresting?"

"They're in the marina," Muller said.

"Narrow it down," Terry said. "There are about five thousand boats in that harbor."

"This one is tied up in Basin D, just off Admiralty Way, right next to a little spot called...are you ready for this? *Mother's Beach*."

"Just when you start to worry that your mass murderer may have lost her sense of humor, Amanda comes through like a comedy champ," Terry said.

As much as I'd have liked to leave Kilcullen at the tar pits, he followed us to the car. There was no stopping him. He was the only horse Deputy Mayor Mel Berger had in this race, and I'm sure he was tagging along to keep me from beating Egan Granville to a bloody pulp.

At least he made himself useful. With a single phone call to CHP, he cleared a straight path along the 10, the 405, and the 90, and we made the twenty-five-minute drive to Marina Del Rey in less than eight.

Guns drawn, we ran to the exact spot Charlie Brock had texted us. Terry held up a hand and pointed at a fifty-foot Bayliner with the name Amanda D painted on the stern.

We boarded, and I banged on the cabin door. "LAPD. Lose the gun, Dr. Dunbar."

"I don't have it," she yelled back. "Granville has it."

"What the fuck?" Kilcullen said. He barked into his radio. "Muller, we're on deck. What's going on down below?"

"She's telling the truth, boss," Muller said. "Granville has the gun."

"How the hell did that happen?"

"She gave it to him. Said that she got what she came for, and she slid the gun across the table to him calm and cool as a blackjack dealer who hears 'hit me.'"

"Is she out of her mind? She just got the son of a bitch to own up to God knows how many counts of felony murder. If any of the shit we just heard sticks, he'll spend the next dozen lifetimes in prison. The only reason to give him the gun is if she has a death wish."

"She's got terminal cancer," Terry said. "She's dying anyway. Granville's confession may or may not hold up, but if he shoots her in cold blood now, it's open and shut, and she wins."

"Muller," I yelled. "Is the camera still rolling?"

"Hell, yeah. And my best guess is you've got six or seven million people glued to the action, and now that we may have an on-camera murder we're on track to break the record that Austrian skydiver pulled when he did that twenty-four-mile free fall a couple of years ago."

I pounded on the cabin door. "Granville," I yelled. "This is Detective Mike Lomax, LAPD. I'm coming in. You'd be wise not to shoot me."

I opened the door and walked down a short flight of steps.

Terry and Kilcullen were right behind me.

The scene was exactly what I'd seen on the monitor in the mobile command post, except that the cabin was much more spacious than the camera had been able to pick up. That, and the 9mm Glock was in Granville's hand, not Amanda's.

She looked at me, her eyes filled with compassion. "Once again, I am sorry for your loss, Detective Lomax," she said. "After I found out who you were, I was able to go back into your wife's medical history. If Ovamax had been pulled off the market when I gave the first warning, she'd still be alive."

I pointed my weapon at Granville. "Put the gun down, Mr. Granville."

"To what end, Detective?"

"I don't know. Justice comes to mind. Whatever you did, you're entitled to more than what Dr. Dunbar just put you through. It's called the Sixth Amendment, Mr. Granville. You have the right to a public trial and an impartial jury."

"Impartial?" He laughed. "I think Dr. Dunbar has successfully beaten the impartiality out of every reasonable human being on the planet. Why don't we just skip the trial and give the public what they want. That's why she gave me the gun, isn't it?"

He put the barrel under his chin, and I felt my body go limp. It was Calvin Bernstein in Dr. Kraus's office all over again. "Don't," I said without any of the compassion or concern that I'd had for Cal less than a week ago.

And like Cal Bernstein before him, Egan Granville locked his eyes with mine and pulled the trigger.

CHAPTER 58

THIS TIME IT was different. No blood. No brain matter. No sound, except for the hollow click of an empty chamber.

Dumbfounded, Granville stared at the cold gun in his hands. He put the barrel in his mouth and pulled the trigger a second time. Then a third.

"You're a coward, Egan Granville," Amanda said. "And cowards should not be permitted to go gentle into that good night. Did you really think I'd give you a loaded gun and let you take the easy way out?"

He threw the Glock across the room at her. It went wide and clattered across the floor.

"Come on, Detective," Granville yelled as Terry picked it up. "Yours has bullets. Use it on me. You'll be a fucking hero."

Terry stood there stone-faced.

"What about you?" he said, tossing the suicide-by-cop challenge at me. "I'd think you'd be happy to shoot me. I heard your wife was one of the women who died."

Whatever shred of sanity, reason, or pure police professionalism that I had left in my body snapped, and I exploded. "*You heard*?" I screamed, advancing toward him, brandishing my gun at his head.

"Mike!" It was Kilcullen.

I ignored him. "You *heard*, you worthless sack of shit? You don't even *know*? My wife was not *one of the women who died.* Her name was Joanie Lomax, and she was a woman who lived, and laughed, and loved, and made life worth living for everyone around her. She didn't *die*. You murdered her, you money-grabbing weasel, as sure as if you put that gun to her head."

"Look, I'm sorry..."

"You're *sorry*?" I said, my breath shallow, my chest constricted, my face on fire. It was all I could do to not pull the trigger and end his miserable existence. "You got caught, and now you want me to kill you because you don't have the balls to live with your lies? You're right about one thing. There are millions of people out there who would have been happy to watch you blow your brains out. But I'm not one of them, and I'll be damned if the last thing I do before I lock you up is stand here and let you turn my Joanie into just another one of your anonymous statistics. Not this time, motherfucker!"

I holstered my gun, dug into my pocket, and pulled out the letter that Big Jim had put it in my hand on Friday night. Then I turned to the camera. I no longer cared about Granville. I only cared about the hole he had left in my life, and I needed to share that emptiness with a world that would understand my loss.

"Joanie was the kind of woman who could even turn the act of dying into a labor of love, and when she died she left behind a series of letters to help me cope with her passing. I can't begin to count how many times I've read them, always wishing for more. And then, two days ago, just hours before the second anniversary of her death, Joanie blindsided me. Another letter arrived.

"I had just announced to my family that I was adopting an eight-year-old girl, and my father gave me this letter that Joanie had written to help me celebrate that moment."

I unfolded the letter, and my hands trembling, my voice unsteady, I began to read.

Dearest Mike,

I'm of mixed emotions as I write this. Bummed like crazy, be-

cause I know I have to be dead in order for it to be delivered, but thrilled out of my mind, because it means that you are about to realize a dream.

When you and I first decided to have a baby there was a story I wanted to tell you, but I decided to wait until I got pregnant. And then, with each failure, my story, which I knew would make you laugh, became sadder and sadder.

But now that you're about to become a father I can finally share it with you, and the only sad part will be that I won't be there to see your face light up when you hear it.

Remember my Aunt Sally and Uncle Barney? Not only did my four cousins and I adore them, but so did every kid in the neighborhood. There was something magical about the way they interacted with children. Never judging, never talking down, always encouraging.

When I was eight years old, Grandma Stockton came from Indiana and spent a week with us. That first day she walked into my bedroom where I was building some fantastic make-believe city out of blocks. She looked around and said, "Where are your dolls?"

I was so screwed. Grandma was always sending me dolls, but I had no interest in them, and they'd go right into my closet. Sometimes I never even took them out of the box. I couldn't lie to her, so I opened the closet, and it was like I had brought her to Barbie's secret graveyard. She was horrified.

She asked me why I didn't play with them, and I said blocks were more fun. She said, "Do you want to have babies when you grow up?" I hadn't really thought about it—I mean I was only eight—but I said sure. And Grandma said, "How do you expect to learn to be a good mommy unless you start practicing now?"

It was probably the dumbest parenting advice ever handed down from one generation to another, but you know me. Even as a kid I did not suffer fools lightly. So I said, "Granny, do you think Uncle Barney is a good father?" Her face lit up. She had three sons, but everyone knew Barney was her favorite. She said, "Your Uncle Barney is the best father in the world. You'd be a lucky young lady to find a husband like him."

I couldn't argue with her, because everybody thought he was such a great dad, so I looked her straight in the eye and said, "Does it just come natural, or when Uncle Barney was a kid, did he practice with a bunch of stupid dolls?"

The old girl shut up, walked out of the room, and that was the last parenting lecture she ever gave me.

Mike, you and Uncle Barney have a lot in common. You're warm, caring, compassionate, understanding, and trust me—I checked with your father before I agreed to marry you—when you were a kid you didn't play with dolls either.

Congratulations on becoming a dad. I'm sorry I can't be there to share the joy with you, so let me share one more memory from my childhood—a quote from the world's most quotable teddy bear, Winnie the Pooh.

"If there ever comes a day when we can't be together, keep me in your heart. I'll stay there forever."

I love you,

Joanie

"That's the woman you decided was worth sacrificing so you could keep filling your pockets with money you're never going to be able to spend," I said to Granville, folding the letter and putting it back in my pocket.

"I don't know how many people are out there going through the same pain you put me through," I said, "but I do this on behalf of every one of them."

I hauled him to his feet, put his hands behind his back, and snapped the cuffs on hard.

"Egan Granville," I said, the tears spilling over and streaming unashamedly down my cheeks, "you are under arrest for the murder of Joanellen Stockton Lomax. You have the right to remain silent. Anything you say..."

PART FOUR
C.T.W.

CHAPTER 59

IT HAD BEEN a week since Diana and I last found the time or the emotional wherewithal for sex, and we were both on fire. After a quick dinner and an inexpensive but highly effective bottle of red at our favorite Italian restaurant, we passed on the manager's offer of dessert on the house, and made a beeline for the parking lot.

As soon as I got behind the wheel, she leaned over and began kissing my neck. "You're a cop," she said. "Run the lights."

"I realize we're in a hurry, but it's totally against the law to—"

She reached down, cupped me between my legs and began massaging with an expertise that made all protests moot.

"Fuck the law," I said, hitting the gas.

As soon as we got home, she stuffed some cash into the babysitter's hand and sent her on her way with the speed of a junkie scoring an eight ball. We checked on Sophie, then clawing at each other like a couple of teenagers in heat, we worked our way to the bedroom.

There's a faded gray armchair parked on one side of the room that basically serves two purposes. It's where I toss my clothes when I'm too tired or lazy to hang them up, and it's Diana's go-to spot for one of the more popular positions in the *Kama Sutra*.

As soon as I locked the door and put my gun on the dresser she unbuckled my belt, pulled my pants and shorts down to my ankles, put one hand to my groin, and pushed me onto the chair. She was in command, and foreplay was not on her agenda.

She lifted her skirt, pulled off her panties, and mounted me. I was hard, she was wet, and I slipped inside of her effortlessly.

She dug her nails into my shoulder blades, parted my lips with her tongue, and gyrated her hips, up and down, back and forth, her body dictating the rhythm of our lovemaking and the intensity of her orgasm. I was practically done before I started, but I held on until her head and shoulders jerked back once, twice, at least five times, and her jaws clenched as she stifled the moans and screams that would have rocked the house had Sophie not been asleep in the next room.

And then came the tears. "Don't you ever fucking do that to me again," she said, her fists pounding hard against my chest. "Ever."

I didn't have to ask what *that* was. "I'm sorry. I was trying to spare you the—"

"Don't you fucking apologize to me and then try to backpedal with an explanation. We are either in this together, or we're not. You don't get to decide what information you share and what information you hold back."

"You're right. I'm wrong. I'm sorry," I said. "I love you. I want to spend the rest of my life loving you. I want to marry you."

"And I want to marry you, but not if you behave like an asshole."

"Behaving like an asshole is a time-honored tradition among the men in the Lomax family," I said, "and Big Jim has set the bar high for his two sons."

She laughed. "I know."

"But I promise I'll do my best. So let me repeat the question. Diana Trantanella, will you marry me?"

The tears started to flow again, and she buried her face in my chest and sobbed. "We've both lost so much," she whispered once she caught her breath and was able to speak.

Diana's husband had died a year before Joanie. We were both aching on the night Big Jim decided that we belonged together, and although I hated to give the intrusive son of a bitch credit, it turned out he was right. Diana and I had healed one another.

"And now you're crying because you're afraid we're going to lose what we have," I said.

"No. I'm crying because we *have* what we have. We're not losing anything."

"So can I take that as a yes on the 'will you marry me' question?"

"Yes, yes, yes, yes, yes."

She kissed me gently on the lips and began to undulate her hips slowly. I was still inside of her, and within seconds I caught her rhythm.

"One more apology," I said.

"Mmmm," she moaned.

"I always thought that when it came time to propose, I'd get down on one knee."

She laughed. "If anyone asks," she said as she picked up the pace, "let's just tell them you did."

CHAPTER 60

I WENT TO bed that night happier than I'd been in years. As I drifted off, wrapped in Diana's arms, reveling in my post-coital afterglow, thoughts about my impending doctor visit began to creep in, and within seconds my euphoria was shrouded by the shadow of death.

I tried to shake it off, and the best I could do was flash back to what Sophie had said the night Grandma Xiaoling died. *We all die, Mike. The best thing to do is have as much fun with your life while you can.*

Thinking back, her world view pretty much lined up with what Charlie Brock had said at the Living With Dying meeting.

"So let's recap," Terry said the next morning. "First you find out that you may have a life-threatening illness. Then instead of waiting for the test results, you adopt a kid, propose to your girlfriend, and now you're worried that dying will put a major crimp on your ability to take care of them."

"It sounds dumb the way you say it, but yeah—that about sums it up."

"Well, you're in luck," Terry said. "We're going to have a sit-down with Amanda Dunbar, and from what I remember about those Chilton-Winslow annual reports there are still half a dozen targets she didn't get around to killing yet. At a half a million a pop that could really add up for you."

Amanda waived her right to counsel. "I have no desire to remain silent," she said. "This company has been lying to the public for years, and it's time to get it all out in the open."

She then spent the next four hours with me, Terry, and Anna DeRoy from the DA's office giving up every detail of the conspiracy to hide the truth about Ovamax, along with the names of all fourteen of the people involved in the cover-up. It included the six she'd had murdered, six more Chilton people, a senior official at the FDA, and of course, Egan Granville.

But she drew the line at helping us track down her paid assassins, Charlie Brock, Rupert Simms, and the pilot we only knew as Dahlia.

"If you're such a champion of justice," Anna said, "why don't you help us bring them to trial? Don't you think the families of the people they murdered deserve that much?"

"Nice try, counselor," Amanda said. "Charlie, Dahlia, and Rupert will be dead soon enough, and if there's any justice in the world, when they get to heaven Saint Peter himself will open the gates and welcome them in."

"As long as we're on the subject of dying," Anna said, "my office is going to vet everything you said here today, and if it holds up, we're going to arrest and prosecute some very prominent individuals."

"I wish I could be around to see it, especially since I'm one of their victims," Amanda said, rubbing a hand over her bald head. "But the odds don't look promising."

"I'm sorry," Anna said, "but your testimony is going to be critical to our case."

"I've got three months at the most, Ms. DeRoy. You put me in front of a video camera, and I'll give you everything you need under oath. My goal was to kill every last one of those fuckers, but putting them in prison isn't a bad fallback position."

"Thank you," Anna said. "I think we're done for now."

"I've got one question for Dr. Dunbar," I said.

Amanda nodded.

"I dug into Egan Granville's background this morning," I said. "He was born into money."

"Lots of it," Amanda said.

"His wife is wealthy in her own right, they have no children, they support several charities, and based on his published net worth he would have been the richest person in the President's cabinet ten times over."

"What's your question?"

"Why? Why would he keep the product on the market once he knew women were dying? And don't tell me he did it for the money. I know some people can never have enough, but I don't buy that he's one of them."

She stared at me, and a trace of a smile crossed her lips. "You're very perceptive, Detective Lomax. You're right. The company stock soared, and that made him look good to investors, but that's not what drove him."

"Then what?"

"Limelight. It started about a year after I reformulated Ovamax. We didn't know the downside yet, but the pregnancy rate was up. That's when *Time* magazine did a feature on Granville. His picture was on the cover, standing in the middle of a hospital nursery, surrounded by newborns. They called him The Baby Maker.

"He loved it. The media has always focused on the ugly side of Big Pharma—unfair pricing, ungodly profits, deceptive test results. Suddenly, in an industry where there are no heroes, Egan Granville was a rock star.

"And then the ovarian cancer numbers started to come in. What I told you when we spoke last week was only partly true. Wade Yancy and everyone involved in the cover-up did it for the money. Not Egan. He could have pulled the plug, but by then he was on everybody's 'A' list, and he was afraid the media would knock him off his pedestal. Fame is a powerful aphrodisiac, and he was hooked."

She leaned across the table. "I'm sorry for your loss, Detective Lomax. I never wanted to meet the families of any of the women who died, because no matter how much I try to disown what happened, it was my product that caused the deaths. But I'm glad I met you... and your wife Joanie."

And then she extended her hand.

Deep down inside of me I'm sure I was quietly grateful for Amanda Dunbar's decision to take the law into her own hands. Without her I might never have known that my wife was a murder victim, and I certainly could not have brought the killers to justice. But Dunbar was a murderer herself, a vigilante whose actions flew in the face of everything Terry, Anna, and I believed in.

I stood up, ignored her hand, and left the room.

CHAPTER 61

THERE WERE FLOWERS on the dining room table, champagne in the ice bucket, and homemade *cannelloni di carne* in the oven.

"I thought your shift went till five," I said to Diana. "How did you manage to pull all this together by six?"

"I only worked half a day. I had a few personal errands to run, and I decided that as long as I had the time, I'd do something special for dinner. It'll be ready in ten minutes. Can you please go upstairs, tear Sophie away from her computer, and ask her to wash up?"

I opened the champagne first, poured two glasses, and carried mine up the stairs. Sophie was at her keyboard.

"You writing a story?" I asked.

"Nope. A letter."

"To who?"

"Jeremy."

"Your father?"

She threw me a cold hard stare. "He's not my father, he's never been my father, but Big Jim says that Jeremy is going to try to get custody of me, so I'm writing to tell him that LAPD Detective Mike Lomax has it covered, so back off."

"Well, that sounds like it's going to take some time to craft, so how about you put it down for now, and finish writing it after dinner."

We washed up and went downstairs.

"It looks fancier than usual," Sophie said.

"Thank you for noticing," Diana responded. "How was school?"

"A little weird, but kind of cool."

"How so?"

"Some of the teachers were talking about Mike. They said he caught some bad guys, but they wouldn't give me any of the details."

"That's because the details are R-rated, and you're still a PG kid," Diana said. "Which means you are absolutely forbidden to search the Internet for specifics about the arrest."

Sophie put down her fork and held up both hands. "Okay, okay, chill. I know the rules."

Diana sipped her champagne. "We have some interesting news for you," she said.

"Lay it on me."

"Mike and I have decided to get married."

Her face lit up. "Really?"

"Really," I said.

"Awesome. Can I be in the wedding?"

"Sure," Diana said. "Would you like to be the flower girl?"

"I've never been to a wedding. What do I have to do?"

"You get to wear a beautiful new white dress, then you scatter rose petals along the bridal path before I walk down the aisle."

"Why?"

Diana shrugged. "It's a tradition, but I have absolutely no idea why." She looked at me for help.

Somewhere in my vast storehouse of worthless information I knew exactly why. The flower girl's white dress is a symbol of purity, and the red rose petals represent fertility. Essentially Sophie was being recruited to depict Diana's loss of innocence in exchange for a life of romance and a fruitful womb.

It was definitely not a subject I wanted to pursue. Not with an eight-year-old. Not with anybody.

"Basically you throw the rose petals to ward off evil spirits," I said.

"Cool," Sophie said. "Just one question—who cleans them up?"

Diana laughed. "Not you. You want the job?"

"Totally. When's the wedding?"

"We haven't figured that out yet. We haven't told anyone except you. We're going to tell the family tomorrow night when we have dinner at Big Jim's."

"Do you think Big Jim and Angel would come to my school next month?"

"What's the occasion?" I said.

"Grandparents Day. I know they're not technically my grandparents, but you're adopting me, so ..."

"Are you kidding?" I said. "Of course they'll come. Getting them there will be easy. Getting them to leave is a whole other problem."

"Can I call them after dinner and ask them?"

"Wouldn't you rather wait till tomorrow night and ask them in person?"

"No. I'd rather do it tonight. I'm the kind of person who likes to get all her trucks in a row."

"Sweetie, I think you just heard the expression wrong," Diana said. "People who are organized get their *ducks* in a row."

"I don't know any people who have ducks," Sophie said. "Do you?"

Diana shook her head. "No."

"Neither do I. But I do know this guy in Riverside who has a gigantic garage. And do you know what he keeps in there?" Sophie said with all the finesse of a trial lawyer about to skewer a witness.

Diana grinned. "Trucks."

"And he's got them all in a row," Sophie said and triumphantly stuck her fork into her cannelloni.

I felt the joy spread to every inch of my being. Suddenly I was getting another shot at the dream. Now there was only one thing standing between me and the life I thought I had lost forever when Joanie died.

A lab report that would be on Dr. Abordo's desk at eight o'clock tomorrow morning.

CHAPTER 62

"WHAT'S GOING ON?" Sophie said as soon as the three of us got in the car.

"What's going on about what?" I said, playing dumb.

"Duh. I thought we had this finely tuned, well-oiled machine. Diana goes to work in her car, you and I go in your car."

I waited for her seatbelt to click, then pulled out. "Diana and I have something to do this morning."

"Wedding stuff?" she said, putting enough topspin on it to make it sound girlishly romantic.

"Life stuff," I said.

"Nice way to dodge a kid's questions, Detective Lomax."

"A kid who never stops asking questions," I said.

"Get used to it. You're stuck with me."

"It's a two-way street, kiddo. You're stuck with us."

"That reminds me," she said, digging into her backpack and pulling out an envelope. "Can you give this to Big Jim?" She handed it to Diana.

"It's addressed to your father," Diana said.

"Jeremy is not my father. I addressed it to him, but Big Jim is going to deliver it in person."

"And who decided that?" I said.

"Me and Big Jim. When I called him last night I told him about the letter, and he said it would be more effective if he gave it to

Jeremy face to face instead of putting it in the mail. He told me to give it to you, and he'll get it from you later on today. Are we cool?"

We were not cool, and Diana rested her hand on my knee to calm me down.

"Big Jim told you he's going to have a face-to-face with your fath—With Jeremy," I said.

"Correct. He'll do it today, and then when we go to his house for dinner tonight, he'll let us know if Jeremy is willing to back off on this custody deal."

Sophie has a way with words, but 'back off on this custody deal' had Big Jim's paw prints all over it.

"The envelope isn't sealed," Diana said.

"Big Jim told me to leave it open. He wants to read it."

"Can we read it?"

"Yes, but wait till I get out of the car."

Diana smiled. "I'm guessing you don't want any feedback."

"Not on this."

As soon as we dropped Sophie off at school I exploded. "Which part of 'don't meddle' did my father not understand?"

"My best guess would be the 'don't' part," Diana said.

"You're almost as funny as the kid," I said. "Read me the letter."

She pulled a single sheet of yellow paper out of the envelope. "It's short and sweet," she said. "Only half a page."

"Half a page is short, but not necessarily sweet. Just read it."

"Okay, calm down," she said. "'Dear shithead.'"

I laughed out loud. "All right, you're funnier than the kid."

"High praise. Now take a long deep breath."

I did as instructed.

"Repeat if necessary while I read the letter," she said.

I inhaled deeply and exhaled slowly. "Go for it," I said.

Dear Mr. Jeremy Tan, I know you were married to my mother when I was born, but that doesn't mean you're my real father.

Real fathers don't leave their kids when they're only six months old. Real fathers play with their kids. They take them to cool places and do fun things with them. They make them pancakes on the weekends, tuck them in at night, and chase after them with a thousand police cars if the kid ever runs away from home.

I wanted a real father all my life, and now I finally have one. His name is Detective Mike Lomax, and we laugh a lot, and he teaches me cool stuff, and he reads all my stories. He's the best father a kid could ever have, so please do not try to get custody of me and take him away. Thank you. Sophie Tan.

P.S. After I get adopted I'm changing my last name to Lomax.

My eyes were watery, and I wiped them. "You're right," I said. "Short and sweet."

CHAPTER 63

DR. ABORDO'S WAITING room was empty. He'd agreed to come in early to accommodate my cop schedule.

There was no receptionist, so I scribbled my name on the top line of the sign-in sheet and sat down.

"It's a good thing you're just here for a consult," Diana said.

"Why's that?"

"Because if they took your blood pressure, they'd call 911. Sophie really got to you."

"It wasn't just her. It was the one-two punch combination of the precocious kid and the meddling old man."

"You heard what the kid said. Get used to it. You're stuck with her."

"I'm stuck with all of you," I said. "Hopefully, for a long time."

The door to the inner sanctum opened, and Dr. Abordo stepped out. "Mike. Come on in."

He was smiling. I took it as a good sign.

The three of us went into his office, and I introduced him to Diana.

"Did he follow doctor's orders over the weekend?" Abordo asked her.

"He didn't tell me you gave him any orders," she said.

"Oh, I did, and I was very specific. Do just what you always do, enjoy life, and have fun."

"He asked me to marry him this weekend, and we decided to adopt an eight-year-old girl, which is not exactly doing what he always does. But he got the fun part down right."

Abordo congratulated us, opened his iPad, and pulled up a lab report. "Let me start with the good news. There is no sign of Philadelphia translocation, which is the specific abnormality of chromosome 22 I was most concerned about."

"Does that mean no Chronic Myeloid Leukemia?" I said.

"I've definitely ruled out CML."

Diana let out a long sigh and squeezed my hand.

"That sounds like the good news," I said. "Somehow I feel you're going to follow it up with some not-so-good news."

He nodded. "Only about ten percent of leukemias are CML, so I have to ask myself what's going on with Mike's white blood cells. These guys are your infection fighters. They grow and divide whenever your body needs them, but your white blood cells are out of whack. My job is to figure out why."

"How do you do that?"

"For starters I want to take a long, hard look at your family medical history."

"I gave you all that last week."

"The intake forms only scratch the surface. Now I'm digging for something deeper. The good news is you're perfectly healthy. No fever, weight loss, bone pain, fatigue—none of the symptoms of leukemia. Except for the high WBC and an enlarged spleen you're in great shape. The next logical step would be to rule out familial neutrophilia."

"That sounds deadly," I said.

"Not at all. In fact it would be the best possible outcome. Familial neutrophilia is genetic—an inherited mutation of the CFS3R gene."

"Could you repeat that minus the mumbo and the jumbo?" I said.

He laughed. "Sorry. Less than two percent of Caucasians have elevated white blood counts, but for them, it doesn't indicate any infection. It's normal. But it's a hereditary condition. Have either of your parents ever mentioned it?"

"My mother died of congestive heart failure seven years ago, and my father would never talk about things like that."

"I guess he's one of those strong, silent, Clint Eastwood types."

Diana laughed out loud. "Just the opposite. Mike's father is an in-your-face, talk-your-ear-off, Donald Trump type, who is an expert on anything and everything."

"There's only two things he doesn't talk about," I said. "His golf score and his health. He's six four, three hundred pounds, and he'd like the whole world to think he's invincible. I know he's had a few incidents of atrial fibrillation, but if there are any other skeletons in his closet he hasn't told me."

"Do you think he'd be willing to come in and go over his medical history with me?" Abordo asked.

"Willing? The man would jump at the chance to get involved in my personal life. I'll have him call for an appointment. What do I do till then?"

"Same advice as last time. Enjoy your life, and this time may I add enjoy this wonderful woman and your new daughter."

CHAPTER 64

DIANA WAITED UNTIL we were in the parking lot before she wrapped her arms around me and gave me a teary-eyed hug. "Thank God," she said.

"I'm not out of the woods yet," I said.

She stepped back. "Mike, you're out of the graveyard. Now call your father and ask him if he knows anything about this white blood cell condition."

"Bad idea."

"Why?"

"Because it's a touchy subject, and you can't pin him down on the phone. *Gotta go, Mike, Angel needs me. Call you back, Mike, one of my trucks need a tow.* No thanks. It can wait till tonight. It'll be harder for him to dodge the question if I catch him off guard, and I'm looking him straight in the eye."

Terry pulled into the parking lot. "There's your ride," she said. Then she waved and gave him a thumbs-up.

I gave her the keys to my car, she kissed me goodbye, and got behind the wheel. "I love you," she said.

"I love you too." I watched her drive off, and I got into Terry's car.

"Diana looked happy," he said. "I'm guessing the doc gave you some good news."

"Not exactly good, but promising. He's hoping it's some genetic blood disorder that's not life threatening. I'm going to my father's house tonight to see if I can dig into his complete medical history."

"Sounds like a fun evening. Wish I could be there, but I'll be out celebrating Egan Granville's latest appointment as Secretary of Laundry at San Quentin State."

"What's the latest on our boy Egan?"

"I just spoke to Anna DeRoy on the way over here. He's singing like Plácido Domingo on opening night at the Met, and he's giving up everybody connected to the crime. There are at least a dozen more doctors across the country that Dunbar didn't know about."

When we got to the station Eileen Mulvey was waiting for us at the front desk. "Gentlemen," she said, "have I told you lately how much I enjoy being your personal assistant?"

"It's every cop's dream job, Mulvey, and you're lucky to have it," Terry said. "What've you got?"

"A package and a warning." She handed Terry a large box.

There was a note taped to it. He tore it open and read it. "*Detective Biggs, You were right about Granville, so while I'm eating crow, you can munch on these. Respectfully yours, Deputy Mayor Mel Berger*."

He opened the box. It was a case of Skittles. He grabbed half a dozen bags and tossed them to Mulvey. "Congratulations. You just won Employee of the Month. Give one of them to Kilcullen. Tell him he was the runner-up. What's the warning?"

"It's for Lomax," she said looking at me. "Your father is waiting for you in the squad room."

"My father?"

"Large man, rather pushy, overbearing actually," Mulvey said.

"That's him. Did he say what he wants?"

"Yes. He wants you." She pointed at the door, and Terry and I went inside.

Big Jim's voice thundered across the squad room. "Where the

hell have you been?"

It wasn't part of the plan, but now was as good a time as any. "Let's do this in private," I said, pulling him into an interview room and shutting the door. "I was at the doctor's office."

"You okay?"

"He can't say yet."

"What's wrong?"

"My white blood count is high."

He shook his head. "You're fine. Just ignore it."

"What do you mean ignore it?"

"*My* white blood cell count is high. My *father's* white blood cell count was high. I don't know if my grandfather ever had a blood test, but he lived to be ninety-seven. It's called familial something or other. It runs in our family."

"Familial neutrophilia?"

"That's the one. Trust me, it's nothing. Hey, look; I can see you're busy, so I'll make it fast. I just swung by to pick up the letter Sophie wrote to Jeremy."

"You just *swung by*, did you? Damn it, Dad, I thought I told you to stay out of that pissing contest."

"You did. And I obeyed. But then—" He shrugged his shoulders and gave me his most angelic Catholic-schoolboy smile—three hundred pounds of pure innocence. "But then my future granddaughter asked me to help. How could I possibly say no on my first shot out of the box as her grandfather? I know you and I had an agreement, but kids trump everything. Am I right?"

"So this is your latest bullshit?" I said. "You'll still keep meddling, but now you'll use Sophie as an excuse."

"Mike, I can see this doctor has got you upset with this whole blood count business, but it's nothing to worry about."

"Nothing to worry about? *We have a family history of high white blood counts?*" I said. "Why the hell didn't you tell me?"

"I did."

"When."

"You were in high school. You were taking biology, and you were exploring the mystery of blood or some crap like that, and I told you all about it. I remember you were laughing your ass off when I said the white blood cells are the infection fighters, and Lomax men have more fighters than most guys."

"I'm sure it was a riot when I was fourteen, but did you think about mentioning it once or twice since then? Hell, you repeat everything else a thousand times."

"So now it's my fault for *not* repeating the same shit over and over? Hey, if your blood count was off, why didn't *you* say something to *me?*"

I didn't answer, and he moved in for the kill. "Look, Mike, don't come down on me for getting involved in this thing with Jeremy, and then stick it to me because I minded my own business when it comes to your medical issues."

The argument was over, and I'd chalked up another loss.

"My hematologist would like to meet with you and ask you some questions," I said.

"I'm happy to help. What's his phone number?"

I wrote it down for him.

"Now just give me the letter, and I'll get out of your hair."

I reached in my pocket and pulled out the envelope. "Do you happen to have any of your recent blood test reports you can show my doctor?"

"Recent? Hell, I've got them going back thirty years. One thing about me—I've got all my trucks in a row."

He plucked the letter from my hand, pocketed it without opening it, and walked toward the door. "See you tonight. Six p.m. Don't be late."

CHAPTER 65

FRANKIE AND IZZY picked Sophie up at school, and Diana went straight to Angel and Big Jim's place after work, so I was alone in the car when Dr. Abordo called.

"Your father came to my office this afternoon," he said.

I cringed. "Did he have an appointment?"

"That's the same question my receptionist asked him. He told her it was a medical emergency."

"I hope she told him to dial 911."

Abordo laughed. "She offered to squeeze him into my schedule on Friday, and he leaned across her desk and says, 'Do I look like someone who can be squeezed into anything?'"

"I'm really sorry, doc. The man has no concept of boundaries."

"That was abundantly clear, but I'm not calling for an apology. Whatever else you may say about your father, he's persistent. He parked himself in a chair and told my receptionist he'd be happy to wait there as long as it takes."

"How long before he wore her down?"

"She's as stubborn as he is, but once she told me who it was, I moved him to the head of the line. He handed me a stack of blood tests going back to the days of dot matrix printers, and then he politely informed me what your diagnosis should be."

"And...?" I held my breath.

"You may not have his questionable charm, but you've definitely inherited his white blood count issues. And he got it from his father. I'll want to monitor you on a regular basis, but the good news is there's nothing but good news. Are you with your fiancé and daughter?"

"No. I'm on my way to a family dinner. We're celebrating our engagement and the adoption."

"Well now you have three things to celebrate."

He hung up, and I broke down. I pulled onto the shoulder, and for the third time in less than a week, the tough macho LA cop dissolved into a puddle of tears. And then came the laughter. Hysteria actually. I hit Terry's speed dial on my cell. I was still laughing when he picked up.

"What's so funny?" he said.

"The doc just called. I'm going to live."

"I told you that a week ago. How come I didn't get any laughs?"

"It's all in the delivery, Biggs. I'll see you tomorrow."

"Yeah, I'm going to need some help with a delicate matter."

"What's that?"

"Remember that hot, blond rookie cop that caught you with your ass hanging out in Dr. Kraus's office?"

"Yeah. Dawn Barclay. What about her?"

"I told her you were circling the drain and asked her to be my new partner. Now I'm going to need help breaking the news to her that she's missing out on the opportunity of a lifetime."

"Sorry to screw up your plans," I said. "But I'll be happy to tell her she's going to have to find her own asshole partner. You're mine."

"You've been hanging around with Kilcullen too long," he said. "You're starting to sound like him. Love you, bro."

"Love you too, man."

I hung up and thought about calling Diana. I decided not to. I was only ten minutes away from Big Jim's place, and I wanted to see the look on her face.

I pulled back out onto the highway, and my mind started racing. I was thinking about a subject that I'd been avoiding since my visit to Doug Heller's office eight days ago.

My future.

CHAPTER 66

WHEN I GOT to El Rancho Lomax I was welcomed by the enticing aroma of Mexican cooking that wafted into the yard. Next came the official greeter, Skunkie, who sniffed me up and down with the thoroughness of a drug-detection dog, then wagged his tail in approval.

I went to the kitchen where Angel and Sophie were cooking up a fiesta.

"Congratulations," Angel said, putting down a large wooden spoon and giving me a hug.

"Wow. Terry and I have caught a lot of bad guys in the past," I said. "This is the first time I saw you so excited."

"Who's talking about bad guys? I'm talking about you and Diana getting married."

"It was going to be a surprise. How did you…?"

Angel's eyes darted toward Sophie, then looked away.

I bent down and gave my daughter-to-be a hug. "Diana and I were going to tell everyone at dinner. Are you the one who spilled the refried beans?"

She gave me a loud giggle that was at least a seven on the Sophie giggle meter, which meant that she either liked my bean joke, or she was just buttering up the cop who had caught her red-handed.

"Me?" she said. "I only told Angel. She's the one who blabbed about it to everybody else."

"And everybody is happy," Angel said. "Now take these out and pass them around." She put a platter of mini chicken-and-cheese quesadillas in my hand and sent me on my way.

I went into the living room and was immediately congratulated by Aunt Lucy, Uncle Daniel, Frankie, Izzy, and my father. I took him aside and told him about the phone call from Dr. Abordo.

His response was classic Big Jim. "See? What did I tell you? Nothing to worry about."

Telling Diana was a whole different story. I asked her to come outside and watch the sunset, and then I mumbled something inane about all the sunsets we'd have in the future. It was totally cornball, but it didn't matter. She'd have cried for joy if I'd read the Miranda rights to her as long as I included the part where Dr. Abordo said, "The good news is there's nothing but good news."

We went inside and sat down at the dining room table, which was laden with trays of tacos and enchiladas, bowls of rice and beans, and a big steaming platter of paella in the center.

Big Jim raised his beer glass. "I'd like to propose a toast to the newest family in the Lomax family," he said. "Mike, Diana, and Sophie."

Everyone yelled, "Cheers" and started to drink.

"Hold on, hold on. I'm not finished yet," Big Jim said.

"Of course you're not," Frankie said. "What were we thinking?"

"Sophie," Big Jim said, "As you know, we are a very tight-knit little bunch. We've all been raised on the principle that family sticks together, supports one another, and is there for one another, no matter what. We're there for the good times, and if there are bad times, you know what we do, don't you?"

She grinned. He'd taught her his credo the first day she walked into our lives. "CTW," she said.

Big Jim radiated with pride.

"CTW?" Lucy said.

"Circle the wagons," Sophie said, "and you're either inside the circle shooting out, or you're outside the circle shooting in."

Lucy looked lost.

"Lucy, it was not easy for me to understand when I first signed on to this crazy family," Angel said. "But don't worry. The important thing is that there are no real guns."

"To Sophie," Big Jim said. "Welcome inside the circle."

We all drank, and as soon as Big Jim sat down, Izzy stood up.

"I'd like to make a toast too," she said. "Sophie, you and I have something in common. I was adopted too. My father was a Marine. He was killed in the line of duty before I was born. My mother died when I was only five. And then the most wonderful people in the world adopted me, just like Mike and Diana are adopting you."

"Well said," Big Jim yelled out.

Izzy smiled. "Hold on. I'm not finished yet."

Frankie flashed me a proud smile. It's not every day that someone cuts Big Jim down to size, and my brother was thrilled that his girlfriend did it—and in front of the entire family to boot.

Izzy turned back to Sophie. "There's only one big difference between what you're going through and what I went through. Your mother is still alive, and every time you celebrate your birthday, you'll know you're another year closer to the time you finally see her again." She raised her glass. "Here's to that wonderful day."

Nobody yelled, "Cheers." We all sipped our drinks quietly. Lucy, Angel, and Diana all reached for napkins to dab their eyes.

Big Jim stood up again.

"Dad, you can't top that one," Frankie said. "Let's eat."

"Relax, I don't have another toast. All I have is this piece of paper," he said, pulling it from his pocket. "It's from Jeremy Tan."

He waited to see if someone would tell him to sit down. No one said a word. He was the center of attention and loving it.

"Jeremy has agreed to..." He squinted at the paper, put it down on the table, and dug out a pair of reading glasses from his shirt pocket. "Where was I?" he said, picking up the paper, and milking the moment for all it was worth.

He began reading. "Jeremy Tan has agreed to termination of parental rights." He looked up and smiled at his audience.

"What does that mean?" I said.

He took off his glasses, which were clearly a prop for his performance. "It means that Angel and I are getting a granddaughter, and that you, Mike Lomax, and your lovely bride-to-be, Diana, are now legally free to adopt that beautiful little girl right there."

Sophie let out a shriek, scrambled out of her seat, and wrapped her arms around his neck.

"Wait a minute, wait a minute," I said. "*Legally* free?"

"Well, if you want to get nitpicky about it, you still have to get a judge to sign off on it, but that's a no-brainer. The important thing is that we have *Jeremy's* signature," he said, waving the paper in the air.

"Dad," I said, "how did this happen?"

"What are you—some kind of detective? My new granddaughter wrote a letter, and Jeremy was so moved by it that he couldn't say no."

He passed me the sheet of paper. It was exactly what he said it was. Signed, sealed, and if I know my father, paid for.

I stood up. "Why don't you all start," I said. "Diana and I want to thank Big Jim in private."

I took her by the hand, and the three of us stepped outside.

"Tell us the truth," I said. "You bought Jeremy off."

Big Jim shrugged. "Technically it was money I was going to leave to you when I die, so in reality *you* bought him off."

"That's unconscionable," Diana said.

Big Jim looked hurt. "Do you really think I'm so terrible for bribing him?"

"Oh, God, no. I think Jeremy Tan is a total dirtbag for selling his daughter. But you, Big Jim Lomax, are a dream." She hugged him. "Thank you. Go on inside. Mike and I will catch up in a minute."

Big Jim didn't waste any time. He hustled back to the house.

"You're okay with this?" I said to Diana.

"Am I okay with the fact that you and I are going to be husband and wife and that Sophie is going to be our daughter?" she said. "I'm very okay."

"I'm talking about Big Jim buying Jeremy off."

"I don't care about Jeremy, Mike. And if you do, then you're focused on the wrong person."

"What are you talking about? Who am I supposed to focus on?"

"Carly."

I opened my mouth and nothing came out. She took my hand, walked me toward Angel's vegetable garden, and the two of us sat down on a stone bench. It gave me time to think, but I still didn't know what to say.

"Do you understand what Carly did?" Diana said.

I didn't have an answer.

"She did the same thing Jeremy did. She waived her parental rights."

"Hold on," I said. "I'm not a lawyer, but I know this for certain. All Carly did was give us temporary guardianship."

"That was five months ago. But about two weeks ago she gave up all legal claim to Sophie."

"Where did you hear that?"

"Daniel and Lucy told me the night they got to LA. Carly got wind of the fact that the government might come after her, but Xiaoling was still alive, and Carly refused to leave, even though she knew the risks. So she and the Zhangs went to a lawyer, and she signed a document that paves the way for us to permanently adopt her daughter. Daniel showed it to me."

"It's made in China," I said. "Do you think it'll hold up in California?"

"Considering the circumstances," Diana said, rewarding me with the smile I was angling for, "I'm sure a Family Court Judge like Elizabeth Sneed White will honor it here."

"Why didn't Daniel show the document to me?"

Diana shrugged. "I don't know. Maybe he picked up on the vibe that you weren't exactly ready to talk about adoption."

"Point taken."

"Daniel and Lucy were there when Carly signed the papers. He said she didn't cry. She knew she was legally relinquishing her rights to her daughter, but she told them, 'If I go to prison, I can go knowing Sophie is safe. And no matter how long I'm in, when I get out, the paperwork won't define our relationship. I'll always be her mother. She'll always be my daughter.'"

Once again I was at a loss for words. I swallowed hard.

"So please, Mike, forget about Jeremy, and don't punish your father for doing what he did. If you want a role model for great parenting, think about what Carly did. I only hope that you and I can love Sophie as much as she does."

"Let's give it our best shot," I said.

She took my hand again and we walked back to the house. Inside everyone was eating, drinking, talking, and laughing.

The room exuded joy. The wagons were circled.

ACKNOWLEDGEMENTS

When the movie ends at a Writers Guild screening, it's proper etiquette for industry professionals to remain in their seats while the credits roll.

But in real life (and by real life, I mean twelve-plexes where I can buy two tickets, a medium popcorn, two bottles of water, and a bag of Twizzlers for just a few bucks more than my first semester's college tuition), as soon as the credits flash on the screen, the audience bolts.

It's different with books. A lot of readers find it fascinating to realize how little the author knows, and how dependent he is on others to help him create fiction out of fact.

First and foremost, there are the medical professionals. My friend and personal physician, Dr. Douglas Heller, was there from the beginning and became the role model for the fictional Doug Heller. Dr. Joseph Fetto gave me insights into the dark side of Big Pharma. And the erudite and charismatic Dr. John Froude navigated me through a maze of life-threatening illnesses. This book would not be what it is if it were not for John's infinite knowledge of the world of diseases, and his unflagging patience with my daily phone calls.

My go-to LA cop, Detective Wendi Berndt, now retired, kept me honest about all things LAPD. However, I did take one liberty. Wendi pointed out that because of a departmental reorg, homicide detectives are no longer housed in the Hollywood station. I ignored the changes and opted to keep Mike and Terry where the three of us are most at home.

And thanks to Detective Sal Catapano, NYPD retired, who is on my speed dial and generously fields all my "what would a cop do if" questions.

Legal expertise came from Chief Civil Administrator John McGovern of the Ulster County NY Sheriff's Office, and my good friend Gerri Gomperts, whose lifetime of experience in family law was invaluable.

I also turned to my pilot buddy Dan Fennessey, EMS paramedic Gabriel Diamond, technowhiz Chris Bollerer, and my favorite Marine Bob Beatty for their expertise.

Thanks to my design and production team Dennis Woloch, Kathleen Otis, and Bill Harrison for making this book look so good and for profreding evrey wurd.

To my partners at Amazon, especially Jason Kuykendall and Brian Mitchell, thank you for making it so easy to bring this fifth Lomax and Biggs book into the world.

To my longtime partners in crime, my editor Jason Wood and my agent Mel Berger, thank you for being part of the heart and soul of this book and all things Lomax and Biggs.

Thank you also to my friend and coauthor on the NYPD Red series, James Patterson, who taught me how to keep readers turning pages and whose influence can be seen throughout this book.

And a big hug for Sophie Gilbert. I met Sophie when she was seven years old, and she inspired the character of Sophie Tan. The real Sophie is a teenager now, but her delightfully cheeky younger self continues to make me smile as it flows effortlessly onto the page.

To my wife Emily, thank you for putting up with me. To my kids, Adam and Sarah, thank you for helping mom put up with me. And to my grandson Zach, who can almost do no wrong, I can't wait for you to be old enough to read this book.

If you read the dedication, you know that I've already thanked every Lomax and Biggs fan on the planet for keeping after me to write this book, but some things bear repeating. I will always be grateful for your dogged persistence.

And finally, for my father, Ben Karp, who died when I was a young man, but whose dreams did not die with him—I love you Dad, and after all these years, here's your other two points.

Marshall Karp

—March 14, 2016

THE BIRTH OF LOMAX AND BIGGS

On September 12, 2005, I got the phone call I'd been waiting for all my life. "Marshall," the voice on the other end said, "we'd like to publish your book."

I'm pretty sure I said, "Thank you," and maybe something like, "Wow," but the one thing I'm positive I said was, "Why?"

My new publisher laughed. He understood writers. We're so conditioned to being rejected that we have a hard time coping with acceptance.

"The characters," he said.

"What about the mystery part?" I said, still having difficulty taking "yes" for an answer.

"Oh, I loved the ride," he said, and then went on to cite three twists he never saw coming. "But after reading the first three chapters, I wanted to spend as much time as I could with Mike and Terry. I love them."

A man after my own heart. When I wrote for TV I learned that most people don't tune in to their favorite shows just to watch a plot unfold. They keep coming back because they want the *predictable emotional experience* of being with people they know and love (or hate), or who remind them of people they know and love (or hate).

And then the publisher said something I wasn't ready for. "How soon can you write me another Lomax and Biggs book?"

Another? The line on my bucket list clearly said, *Write Book*. The line after that said, *Learn to Fly Plane*, not *Write Another Book*. But who was I to argue with the world's smartest publisher?

Terminal is the fifth Lomax and Biggs book. I've written each one so that it stands on its own, but the arc of the characters spans the series. So if this was your first taste, you can check out sample chapters of the other books at www.karpkills.com.

And if you're like the man who called to say he wanted to spend as much time as he could with Mike and Terry, the good news is you have four more books to look forward to.

Thank you for supporting my life of crime.

—Marshall Karp

CPSIA information can be obtained
at www.ICGtesting.com
Printed in the USA
LVOW12s2032220416
484898LV00002B/145/P